The Trouble with Tessa

Also by Ofelia Dumas Lachtman

Call Me Consuelo

A Good Place for Maggie

The Girl from Playa Blanca

Leticia's Secret

Looking for La Única

The Summer of El Pintor

The Trouble with Tessa

Ofelia Dumas Lachtman

PIÑATA BOOKS
ARTE PÚBLICO PRESS
HOUSTON, TEXAS

This volume is made possible through grants from the City of Houston through The Cultural Arts Council of Houston, Harris County.

Piñata books are full of surprises!

Arte Público Press
University of Houston
452 Cullen Performance Hall
Houston, Texas 77204-2004

Cover design and art by Giovanni Mora
Chapter and cover illustrations by Rebecca Ellerbroek

Lachtman, Ofelia Dumas.
 The Trouble with Tessa / by Ofelia Dumas Lachtman.
  p. cm.
 Summary: After Tessa's father inexplicably makes her change her summer plans, she spends the summer wondering what he is hiding, experimenting with magic spells, and making a new friend.
 ISBN-10: 1-55885-448-7 (alk. paper)
 ISBN-13: 978-1-55885-448-2
 [1. Secrets—Fiction. 2. Family life—Fiction. 3. Witchcraft—Fiction. 4. Neighbors—Fiction. 5. Hispanic Americans—Fiction. 6. California, Southern—Fiction.]
 I. Title
 PZ7.L13535Tr 2005
 [Fic]—dc22   2004060005
                                                              CIP

5 6 7 8 9 0 1 2 3 4   10 9 8 7 6 5 4 3 2 1

To my son-in-law John.
Thank you for your unflagging interest.

Chapter One

Tessa del Campo sat beside her father in their pickup truck and stared unhappily at the other cars on the road. Her face, under a cap of curly black hair, was puckered up into a frown. She was in a grungy gray mood.

It had begun after they left Lisa at the gate at Los Angeles airport and Tessa realized it was really happening. One of my best friends is going to San Francisco and then to a neat summer camp and I have to stay here in Seagate! She sighed.

Her father said, "I'm sorry about your summer plans, honey. Sorry that we couldn't let you go up north with Lisa, but it couldn't be helped."

"Why, Papá? Why couldn't it be helped? I wish you'd tell me."

"I'm sorry, really I am, but all I can say now is that you'll understand before the summer's over."

"That's not fair! You should tell me now!"

"I would if I could, Teresa. You'll just have to be patient. I know it's not easy. When I was eleven, waiting was hard for me too."

His face was furrowed into a frown as he spoke, but even that did not stop him from being handsome. He had black eyes, a nice strong chin, and curly black hair just like hers. And he always wore white: white shirts with well-pressed khaki pants. But right now she was not

1

thinking how nice he looked. She was mad at him. Doesn't he realize that that kind of stuff doesn't help? Especially with a grungy gray mood. Besides, I'm closer to twelve than eleven!

When they turned onto Grant Street, she stared glumly at her neighbors' green lawns and bright flowers. Green was her favorite color, but today the grass and flowers seemed as colorless as a black-and-white movie. Only the old Duncan house next door looked the same: empty, broken-down, and gloomy.

It did not help her mood that Wendell Timson, the freckle-faced red-haired boy across the street, was waiting for her. The Timsons had lived across the street ever since she could remember, and from preschool through sixth grade Wendell had tagged after her like an extra shadow. Now he got off his bike and said, "Thought you were going to camp with Lisa."

"No, I'm not," she said and gave him an angry look as she ran into the house.

Falling asleep that night was not easy. She was still mad at Papá. He had always been strict, but he had never been unfair before, and that's what *really* bothered her. It wasn't so much that she couldn't go to camp with Lisa. The truth was that she did not like being gone from home that much, especially now that she had discovered something very exciting. But Papá was acting weird and she didn't like that. She twisted and turned and, finally, with the comforting sound of Nana María's and Mamá's voices coming from the kitchen, she fell asleep.

When she awakened the next morning, a bird was singing in the tree by her bedroom window and her old

Raggedy Ann grinned at her from the top of the chest of drawers. Tessa grinned back. Things weren't that bad. She *did* have her special project to look forward to. And she had all summer to work on it. She bounced up in bed as her door swung open and Nita, her seven-year-old sister, stood in the doorway.

"Guess what, Tess!" she said, her black eyes sparkling.

"You call me Tess again, and I'll start calling you Nit— no matter what Nana María says. My name's Tessa or Teresa!"

Nita ignored the threat. "Somebody's moving into the Duncan house!" she shouted, stuck out her tongue, and left.

Tessa jumped out of bed, pulled back the curtains, and looked out the window. A truck was parked in front of the Duncan place. Tools, boxes, and paint cans were scattered on the ground, and two men were hacking away at a gnarled vine that covered the gate.

When the rusty iron gate squeaked open, she groaned and stamped her foot. "That's not fair!" she grumbled. "I'm going to lose my green arbor."

Last year she had found two loose boards on the fence between the Duncan house and the empty lot next door. That's when she discovered a special hideout. It was a rear corner of the Duncan garden covered over with vines and filled with shadows. It was mysterious and, best of all, no one but she knew about it. *But they would after today.* She sighed, a long drawn-out sigh, pulled on her clothes, and went to have breakfast.

The kitchen smelled sweet and spicy. There were two things that her mother liked to do best of all. Cooking was one of them. Playing the piano was the other. Today, Mamá was making an apple pie. Her long brown hair was tied back with a scarf and her cheeks were flushed from the warmth of the oven. Tessa got a box of cereal from the cupboard and a quart of milk from the refrigerator and sat at the table to watch her.

After putting the pie in the oven, Mamá turned and said, "You look glum, Tessa. Missing Lisa?"

"Sure." Pictures of Lisa crossing the Golden Gate Bridge, visiting the zoo, and shopping in a huge store whipped through her mind. "She's lucky. Her father'll take her all sorts of exciting places and buy her a ton of new clothes."

"Then be happy for her," Mamá said. "And don't forget that you have other friends here."

"Oh, sure, there's Haley. But not for long. She's going to her dad's ranch in August. Me, if I want to visit Papá, all I do is walk down Main Street to Del Campo's Hardware and Garden."

"I know," her mother said with a little laugh, "that's what so nice. He's so close."

Tessa put her cereal spoon down. "Mamá," she said. "Why didn't you and Papá let me go with Lisa?"

Her mother threw her a funny look. "Because . . . because your father needs you here. I'm not entirely sure why, but he says I'll know by the end of the summer. Even Nana María doesn't know . . . or says she doesn't know." She smiled. "Oh, yes, Tessa, I tried to coax it out of your grandmother. . . . Well, I'm sure your father has good reasons, even if you and I don't understand them."

Tessa grinned into her bowl of Cheerios. You could never coax anything out of Nana María. Everyone tried at

Christmastime, but Nana María never gave away a secret. And she knew *everything*. She lived in a small house that Papá had built in the "garden," what he called the backyard. And it *was* a garden. Nana María had the place filled with flowers and vegetables, and everything grew for her. Of course, she spent hours helping everything to grow. You could always find her working in the garden in a pair of faded old jeans and a floppy grass hat. She was always there. That's probably why she knew everything.

Tessa pushed her cereal bowl away. "So Papá's not even telling you. That's weird. I know you think he has good reasons, but does that mean he has the right to be unfair?"

"Don't be disrespectful, Tessa. Besides, I don't remember your being all that excited about going with Lisa. You were the one who argued that Lisa was only going to camp because it was convenient for her father."

"I know, I know. But he *does* have to go back to work and there'll be no one to take care of her. And he did want Lisa to be happy. That's why he invited me." She watched her mother roll out the extra pieces of pastry and sighed, thinking of all that she might be missing.

The divorced kids have it so easy, she thought. Look at Haley and Lisa. They get to go to special places with their fathers and grandmothers because their parents are divorced.

"Did you know," she said to her mother, "that Haley's dad sent her scads of money to buy boots? Of course, she needs good boots. A movie star has a ranch right next door to her father's. She'll probably be riding with him a lot."

"Now stop that!" Mamá said. "The trouble with you, Tessa, is that you have a wild imagination."

"It's *not* wild! My imagination is just . . . just special, like it helps me to discover special things. Anyway, it's true about Haley." She paused. "Mamá, can our family do something fun this summer?"

"We are, Tessa. The Seagate Summer Fair begins in just three weeks."

"Ugh. The fair's not what I call fun."

"You used to love it. Have you forgotten the carnival at Council Park? Have you forgotten that I have the bake booth at the fair and that I'm letting you and Nita help?"

Tessa gave up. "No, I haven't forgotten," she said and went back to her room to watch what was going on at the Duncan place.

All day she watched the workmen. In the middle of the afternoon she went out front and sat on the curb, hoping to learn something. One of the men said, "Hello, there," but before she could ask him anything, he grabbed a portable power saw, one just like her father's, and hurried into the house. It was a long day, especially since the workmen did not leave until after dinner. Then, while Nana María was with Mamá in the living room, Tessa tiptoed out of the back door and across the empty lot to the Duncan place.

Once through the fence she paused to look around. Back here everything looked the same. She went straight to a post that held a yellow glass lantern screwed to its top. The glass globe was cracked but still whole and, although the metal ring that held it to the post was rusted, it was still easily moveable. She lifted the globe. Yes, her things were there, still safe.

Carefully, she took out three bird feathers and put them in the plastic bag she had brought with her. A crown made of twigs came next, then a thin branch with glued-on beads.

The last was a small bottle of pink liquid. The rose potion. She shook it hard and nodded. Good. Papá's aftershave lotion kept the rose petals from rotting. She shoved the bottle into the bag and grabbed a small green book. Her diary.

The stone bench and the birdbath were just beyond the lantern. She brushed leaves off the bench and sat down with her diary. This was where she could really be alone. Since she had told Nita that ghosts roamed this garden, her sister did not follow her here anymore. Tessa began to write.

Dear diary,
    If only there were a real ghost here! Then, maybe, no one would move in. And we'd have a *real* mystery too. Papá laughs when I talk about mysteries. He says that the only mystery around here is how Seagate stays a quiet little town with the city of Los Angeles and the ocean squeezing it on all sides. Seagate's quiet, all right. More like bor . . . *ring!* And so is my family. Sure, my mother makes the best enchiladas in the world and Papá builds things and plays a cool guitar, but that isn't like being in television or being an astronaut or maybe even governor. Being the owner of a hardware store and being a mom aren't very exciting things for parents to be. So if there's going to be any excitement in my life, I'm the one who'll have to make it happen.
    I guess I'm getting grungy gray again. But losing the arbor is such a bummer. It's a good thing my magic things are ready.

She paused and looked around, then wrote,

Well, it's getting dark and I've got to say goodbye to everything. I'll see you tomorrow, diary. Somewhere.

She lay her diary and the plastic bag on the bench and slipped around a ragged hedge into the main garden. Fog was spreading over the roof of the old house in a gray blanket, giving it an eerie look. In a U formed by two wings of the house, a movement caught her eye and she drew in her breath, startled. But it was only Homer, her neighbor's skinny white cat, jumping onto a railing. As she turned to go, he leaped to an overhang below the upstairs windows. She gasped. Someone or something white was at the window right above her!

She raced back to the arbor, picked up the plastic bag and ran to the fence. She pushed the loose boards and the scratchy vines aside and dove through. She flew across the vacant lot and even faster across her own backyard. In her room she looked at herself in the mirror and grinned sheepishly. Holy pajamas! Have I begun to believe my own ghost stories? The grin disappeared and a frown took its place. Maybe, she thought and shuddered, maybe I wasn't supposed to shake the rose potion!

Chapter Two

Tessa did not have long to worry about the rose potion before there was a knock on the door. Only one thought remained. Was the potion really that powerful?

Quickly, she stuffed the bag with her magic things into a drawer and called, "Come in." It was Papá. She knew it would be. Mamá and Nana María always knocked but most often did not wait for her to call "Come in." Papá always did.

"There you are, Tessa," he said. "We've been looking for you. We're ready to leave for Lupe's. Where were you?"

"Peeking at the Duncan place to see what they're doing," she said, feeling virtuous because she was telling the truth without giving away her secret.

"We'll know soon enough," he said. "Get a sweater and come on. Your aunt will be waiting."

Lupe, her father's sister, lived near the ocean in an ancient two-story house in the old part of Seagate. About once a week they took dessert to her house. They did that because, as Mamá explained, it was easier for five people, each with two strong legs, to go over there than for Lupe to bring Uncle Jim and his wheelchair to our house. Tonight dessert would be Mamá's apple pie. With ice cream, Tessa hoped. She was sure Lupe (who did not like

9

to be called Tía or Aunt) would have ice cream somewhere in her huge old-fashioned kitchen.

The house Uncle Jim and Lupe lived in had belonged to Uncle Jim's parents and his grandparents before that. It had a big attic that, until recently, had been filled with old things: boxes and broken chairs, old suitcases, and a huge trunk with a rounded top. But not anymore—it had been turned into a small apartment, one that Uncle Jim Smith and Lupe rented out.

Tessa felt a little tugging at her throat as she pulled a sweater from her closet. She'd liked the attic the way it was. Scary, with all the cobwebs and broken things. She shivered a little, thinking of what she'd found there last month.

That was when Lupe had said, "Tessa, if you want anything out of the attic, take it now. Everything will be gone soon."

Tessa had been excited as she thanked Lupe. The old trunk. That's what she wanted to look in. So she had raced up to the attic steps, hoping that Nita, who was playing checkers with Uncle Jim downstairs, would not follow. Tessa found the old trunk near the back wall, the key in the rusty lock. Its lid squeaked and groaned as she raised it. On the very top she found old-fashioned dresses and bundles of buttons and lace. Next came some old books and a pair of funny high-top shoes. As she pulled things out, she noticed a faint sweet smell. It grew stronger as she dragged out the last thing, a heavy velvet coat. All that was left scattered on the bottom of the trunk were a bunch of tattered brownish-yellow pages. Her eyes fell on a page that said "Recipes and Rites for Witchcraft," and her mouth dropped open. Her heart beat fast as she thought, these tell you how to be a witch! And I came directly to the trunk, so I was meant to find them!

She leaned over the edge of the trunk and, stretching her arms, very carefully gathered up the sheets. Then she sat on the floor to read them. But when she heard Nita running up the attic steps, she shoved them into her pocket.

Now, all these weeks later in her bedroom, Tessa grabbed her sweater, yelled, "Coming, coming!" to Mamá's impatient call, and dashed down the hall. They piled into the car and she settled back between Nita and Nana María. She loved the fog. It made shimmery halos around the lights and turned the familiar Seagate streets into alien lands. So long as Nita was not chattering, it was easy to pretend that she was on a far planet.

Lupe, who was round and warm and soft, was waiting for them at the front door of her house. She gave them their usual hugs and led them into the kitchen to help serve the apple pie. And, yes, there was ice cream! It was a fun evening. Papá played the guitar and they sang and then they all sat back to talk. It was when the grown-ups were discussing what was going on at the Duncan place that a thought hit Tessa that tied her stomach into a knot.

She had left her diary on the stone bench in the green arbor. She squirmed at the thought that someone might be reading it. Those were all her private feelings. But more important were the things that she'd copied into her diary from the pages in the old trunk. On the night she had found the pages, they'd started to crumble, so she'd stayed up hours after her bedtime copying them.

She squirmed again and Mamá threw her a warning look. The grown-ups were still talking about the Duncan place, telling what they knew about the new tenants, but she did not want to listen anymore. What she wanted was her diary! After all, she had not even had a chance to try any of the magic spells. Scraping a little branch to make the jeweled wand had taken time, but it was the rose potion that had slowed her down. "For thy potion to possess magic," the yellowed pages had said, "rose petals shall slumber in its depths through one full moon." Two days ago a bright full moon finally had arrived. The rose potion was ready. And now her diary was gone. Tessa sat on the edge of her chair, trying not to fidget.

At last it was time to go home and they all got into the car. All, that is, except for Nana María, who had forgotten her purse again. So she and Lupe went back into the house to get it. Tessa bit her lip impatiently. When Nana María returned and the car was moving, she thought, I'll sneak over and get my diary the minute we get home. On the way home the fog grew so thick that she wondered if she would be able to find her way to the green arbor. But when they all piled out of the car and she could not even see her hand in front of her face, she stopped wondering. She knew she'd have to wait till morning.

Early the next morning when Papá had gone to work and Mamá was in the shower, Tessa slid quietly into the backyard on her way to the Duncan place. But she was not quiet enough to slide by Nana María unseen.

"*Muchacha,*" she called, "*ven acá.*" Nana María always threw in some Spanish when she spoke to them. She was not going to let them forget that language. Now, in English, she said, "Girl, come here," then added, "Help me tie up this tomato plant."

"Only one plant, please, Nana," Tessa said. "Please, please, I have something very important to do."

Nana María pushed her grass hat back on her head, looked at her intently and then nodded. "All right," she said. "Hold this branch against the frame while I tie it and then go. Very important things need quick attention."

"Thank you, Nana," Tessa said and held the branch for her grandmother. When she was through she let herself out the back gate and across the empty lot to the Duncan fence. Except for some drops of water falling from the trees, no one would have known that the fog had been as dismal as dishwater last night. Today the sun was bright; it glistened on the damp leaves. She felt better. Why had she been so worried last night? Her diary would certainly be right where she had left it.

Tessa stepped through the loosened fence boards, walked into the green arbor and her mood plummeted. The stone bench was bare. She fell to her knees and swept away the damp, sticky leaves that were under the bench. No diary. Could she have dropped it when she saw the white thing at the window? She *had* to go see.

Near the old house she stole a look at the upstairs windows. A white painter's cap hung from the frame of one of them. Terrific! That dumb thing was what had scared her. She threw the window an angry glance. She went back to the arbor, searching the ground with her eyes. She swept away more leaves and pulled aside branches until she heard the workmen arriving and then, reluctantly, went home.

After breakfast, Mamá said, "I have your summer job lists, girls."

Tessa groaned and Nita said, "I'm too little to work."

"So I've given you little jobs, Nita. Don't you think that's fair?" Mamá's favorite word was "fair." During the summer, she said, it was fair that Nita and Tessa help more around the house. Papá had agreed. So there was no getting out of it.

Today Tessa had to clean the bedroom mirrors. She hurried through the job. When she was through she hurried to the telephone desk in the hallway and punched in Haley's number. "Something awful's happened," she said when her friend answered. "You absolutely won't believe it, but . . ." Tessa caught a glimpse of Nita listening near the door. "I guess I can't talk right now, after all. Big Ears is around."

"Well, come over right this minute!" Haley said. "I have to know what's happened."

"I can't. Today's my day to help with the lunch dishes."

"Pooh," Haley said. "Well, after lunch'll have to do. Bring a swimsuit."

Haley lived with her mother in a condo in a huge building that had other condos and hallways and stairways and a dozen little courtyards filled with potted plants. It was a building where you could be lost for hours looking for the right door.

At the entrance to Haley's building, Tessa pushed the button above the names Elizabeth Rankin and Haley Star

Rankin and waited. "I'll buzz you in," Haley said over the intercom, "but don't come up. Meet me at the pool."

Haley had long blonde hair and blue eyes that seemed to change color with whatever she was wearing. Today they looked purple because she had on a purple bikini. She came down a stairway to the swimming pool. "What were you talking about on the phone?" she said when they met at the pool. "What could be so bad?"

"Somebody took my diary," Tessa said glumly as they draped their towels on plastic lounge chairs.

"Oh, Tessa. Who would want your diary?"

"I don't know. All I know is I left it next door at the Duncan place and it's gone."

"Tessa del Campo! How could you be so dumb? Look again. It's got to be there somewhere."

"I did and it's not. Personally, I think one of the workmen took it."

"No way. They wouldn't be interested."

"Well, forget it. I had to tell someone and I thought you'd understand."

"I do, really I do. That's why I keep *my* diary under lock and key."

Tessa frowned as she pulled off her shirt and shorts, exposing a two-piece bright blue bathing suit. It was a hip hugger, not a bikini. "Maybe you can have a bikini next year," Mamá had said. But it was *this* year that she wanted one! She stretched out on the lounge and closed her eyes. Lying in the sun felt good, so good that Tessa was close to falling asleep when Haley spoke.

"What are they doing to it?"

"To what? I can't always read your mind, Haley."

"The Duncan place. What else?"

"How'd you know they were doing anything to it?"

"Everybody knows. The only thing I don't know is who's moving in."

That's another trouble with this town, Tessa thought. News gets around faster than the flu. "Well, if you must know, it's an Arab sheik. He has ten wives and twenty children, and they're going to add at least two more floors and—"

"Cut it out, Tessa! I'm tired of your stories."

"That's because you don't have any imagination."

"Whatever. I have all the imagination I need." She bounced up and produced a box of plastic fingernails. "Let's fix our nails."

"Not me. My parents don't even let me wear polish."

"*Really?* They're not very creative, are they?" Quickly, Haley added, "But they're nice and very, very practical."

That's what her parents were, all right, Tessa thought. Practical. Sensible. Mr. Killmeyer, her principal had called them "good, solid people, both feet on the ground, while your head, Teresa, is up in the clouds."

Why couldn't her parents be more like Haley's? Haley's mother was something important in computer design and her father did scientific experiments on his ranch. They were divorced and that meant that Haley had two really special places to live. It also meant that they *always* tried to make Haley happy. Tessa sighed, a long sad sigh, and twisted around on the lounge chair in time to see Haley dump the plastic nails back in their box.

"Betts said it was all right to use them," Haley complained, "but I can't make the dumb things work."

Tessa shook her head. Betts. Imagine being allowed to call your mother Betts. She wouldn't dare call Mamá Claudia.

"Well," Haley said, "if we're not going to have beautiful nails, we might as well get wet. Come on, it'll be fun." She dove into the pool.

Tessa followed her friend into the water. I like Haley's swimming pool, she thought, and I like splashing in the water, but nothing, absolutely nothing's going to be any fun until I find my diary.

Chapter Three

Riding home on her bike, Tessa thought again about her parents. No, I'm not like them. Personally, I think that if I was, I wouldn't believe in magic, and I really do. Especially now. Anyway, I don't care what Mr. Killmeyer said, I'm glad my head's up in the clouds. It's more fun that way.

She grinned as she pumped up a small hill. I'll never forget the look on Wendell's face when I said there were bats in the auditorium ceiling. No matter what Haley and Lisa said, it wasn't a crazy idea. After all, hadn't the newspaper said that they'd blown up a bat cave by the ocean and hundreds of them were looking for a place to hang out? She turned the corner onto Grant Street.

Nita was waiting for her by the Duncan place. She waved her arms and shouted, "Hey, Tess, you missed the whole thing!"

Across the street, white-haired Mrs. Herriot came out on to her porch and poked her head over the railing.

"They moved in!" Nita shrieked. "With tennis rackets and sleeping bags, and they're cleaning out everything! Look!" The workmen's trucks were gone from the street. In their spot was a huge boxlike container, a rented dumpster that was as big as a truck. Nita jumped up and down and pointed at it.

"Stop screeching," Tessa said to her sister. "A deaf man could hear you." She circled around the dumpster then got off her bike and leaned it against a lamppost. Her heart had begun to race. Her diary. It might be in the trash. She waited until Mrs. Herriot went back into her house, then pulled herself up on a side of the dumpster for a look. It was almost empty except for a pile of stained and rotting old boards, a broken wooden chair, and some dusty boxes dumped in a corner.

Nita tugged at the hem of her shorts. "What'cha doing, Tess?"

"Looking. What do you think?" Tessa said, and climbed over the top. "And stop calling me Tess!"

"Okay, okay. What's in there?"

"That's what I'm going to find out."

"Yuck! With all that trash?"

Tessa shrugged and jumped into the dumpster, raising a cloud of dark gray dust. She picked her way across the sticky floor. Gingerly, she nudged the boxes off the broken chair. One by one, she moved the boards until the floor showed. Nothing. Disappointed, she dragged the chair back on top of the old lumber and tossed the boxes after it. She started to hoist herself over the edge of the trash container, but stopped. There was something she'd seen on one of the boxes. Maybe she'd better take another look. She dropped back onto the floor.

The box was black and dusty. In bold letters it said "The Oracle." She blew at the dust, sneezed, and then brushed it off with her hand. Through a cloudy mist painted on the cover, a pair of burning black eyes looked straight at her. "Find answers to all your questions," she read. "Investigate the secrets of telepathy and the unknown." A shiver shot up her spine. An answering board! A magic board! First I found the magic book and now this. It's an omen. I must have special powers. She took a long, shaky breath. Yes! I can feel them pounding in my blood.

With the box under one arm, Tessa climbed onto a rung of the broken chair. She tossed the box onto the grass below her. "Nita," she called, "watch this for me."

Nita knelt beside the box. "O-R-A-C-L-E," she spelled. "What's that?"

"Someone who figures out mysterious things," Tessa said, dropping to the ground.

"Uh-uh-*ah*," Nita singsonged, shaking her head. "That's a detective."

"You know a lot about it," Tessa said. "An oracle *knows* and a detective has to find out."

"What're you going to do with it?" Nita asked.

Tess shrugged. "Don't know yet."

"Then why'd you take it?"

"Because. Because it was put out there for me. There are special powers at work."

Nita climbed onto a little pink bicycle. "I think you're silly," she shouted. "Silly, silly, silly! Tess, Tess, Tess!" She swung her bike around and raced down the sidewalk.

Tessa put the Oracle under her arm and circled her bicycle toward her house. She had a weird feeling that she was being watched. She had taken only a couple of steps when the shrubs behind the old iron fence shook, sending particles of dust flying, and a voice said, "I've been watching you."

Tessa swung around. The Oracle and the bike both fell to the ground with a loud clatter.

A boy with the blackest hair and the bluest eyes she had ever seen came out from behind the shrubs to stand by the rusty gate.

"Is that your dumpster?" she asked.

"Sure is," he said. "What were you doing in it?"

"Looking for something I lost. Not this." She held out the Oracle. "This was thrown out and I . . . I figured nobody wanted it . . . I thought . . ." She fumbled around for words and then stopped.

"Oh, that," he said. "You can have that. That's just some junk from the cellar. What *were* you looking for? A ball or something?"

"No. A book, a little green one. Have you seen it?"

"I'm not sure." The boy shrugged. "Green? No, I'm not sure."

"What do you mean you're not sure? Have you seen it or haven't you?"

"I can't tell you," he said with a grin, "not unless your name is Athena del Campo, a woman of the twenty-first century."

"You've been reading it!" Tessa cried. "I can't believe it. You've been reading it!" Her face was hot and her eyes smarted with angry tears. To hide the tears she bent over to pick up the Oracle. She blinked furiously until the tears were gone. Then, holding her head up high, she turned and said in a haughty voice, "I'm Athena, the goddess of wisdom, and the diary's mine. I'd like you to return it . . . please?"

She was speaking to an empty space. The boy was not there. She hurried to the open gate. The house door, too, was open, but no sound came from within.

"Hey, you!" she called. Then, taking a few steps closer to the house, she yelled, "Hey, you! I want my diary!"

There was no answer.

She waited a few minutes, searching the shrubbery and the open windows with her eyes. Reluctantly, she turned away, went through the open gate and picked up her bike. She kept looking over her shoulder as she walked it slowly to her house. But she saw no one. The boy had vanished as suddenly as he had appeared.

Chapter Four

Tessa heard the music all the way down the driveway to the garage, where she slid the bike into its slot. Her mother was playing the piano. That meant that no one could interrupt her unless it was an emergency. When Mamá played the piano, everyone in the family, except Nita, liked to stop to listen. For instance, right now Nana María, rather than digging in the flower beds, was sitting on a bench in the shade of the lemon tree, her eyes closed and her lips curved in a little smile that made her wrinkled face almost pretty.

Everyone knew that if Mamá had not fallen in love, and if she had not wanted to have children and raise them while she was still not too old, that Mamá might have been a professional, maybe even a concert pianist. But Mamá played only for her family and, sometimes, friends, and especially for herself.

Tessa tiptoed through the house to her room. She closed the door quietly and, dropping the Oracle on the floor, flopped down on her bed. There was no use in trying to hide it. The fact was that she was madder at herself than at the black-haired boy. Why hadn't she asked for her diary right away, instead of giving him a chance to disappear? Well, it was too late to worry about that. What she was going to do now is have a glass of water, go back and find that guy wherever he was, and get her diary.

Her plans were ruined when she threw open her front door and saw the black-haired boy and a man with black hair just like his drive away in a dark gray sports van. Her shoulders sagged. She would not see her diary tonight. She felt even worse when Wendell Timson caught sight of her and yelled, "Hey, Tessa, that's the new guy. They're gonna move in in a couple of days."

She stepped out onto her porch and watched Wendell cross the street. "What do you mean a couple of days?" she asked when he came up her walkway. "They've already moved in."

"Nah, Tessa. Where've you been? Mark says they're moving in day after tomorrow, or maybe the day after that." Wendell grinned, a big broad grin, and some of his freckles rearranged themselves on his face. "He's my friend already . . . I think. Anyway, he told me his name."

"Big deal," Tessa said crossly. Then, because she realized that she was taking her bad mood out on him, she said, "That's nice, Wendell. Guess I'd better go in now."

In her room she took her ill humor out on the Oracle. She kicked it under her bed so hard that it thumped the wall on the other side of her bed. She was cross all evening, too cross to talk, not even bothering to call Nita "Nit" when she kept calling her "Tess."

The weather the following morning didn't help. It was raining. It wasn't supposed to rain in summer. It *never* rained in summer. But it was. And it rained all day. Still, the day turned out to be better than Tessa had anticipated.

Nana María, Mamá, Nita, and Tessa made mountains of cookies. They made three different kinds: chocolate chip, big puffy oatmeal with raisins, and fudge brownies. Most of them went into the freezer for the Seagate Summer Fair's bake booth, but there were two plates full for the family.

When Haley called to complain about the weather, Tessa had a great idea. "I know it's not beach weather, Haley," she said. "But who cares? We have something better to do!" Tessa went on to tell her about finding the Oracle and then a little bit about the boy called Mark.

"How old is he?"

"How would I know? Twelve, maybe."

"What's he like?"

"He's okay, I guess. But forget him. Personally, I think it's the Oracle that's important. We can ask it all sorts of things."

"Like what?"

"Well, I'm going to ask when I'm going to Paris and . . . and what I should call my first novel."

"That's silly. But, okay, if it's still drizzling tomorrow, I'll come see your old oracle."

That same night at bedtime Tessa sat on her bed staring at the light and shadows made by the lamppost and the elm by her window. She sighed. *I promised my diary to make something happen this summer. But what? Mamá's idea of excitement is the fair. But there's nothing exciting about a bake booth, even if the cookies were scrumptious. If Mamá was into technology like Haley's mother, it might be different. Then, maybe she'd be in charge of all those special computer games.*

Tessa twisted uncomfortably. The squirmy feelings were guilt. Mamá's okay. I guess she can't help it if she likes to cook. She likes books, too, and she *is* smart. She's the one who said I should be a writer because of my imagination. Anyway, as to what I promised my diary, the Seagate Summer Fair is absolutely not it.

The next day Tessa and Haley sat facing each other on two chairs in Tessa's bedroom, their knees touching. The magic board called the Oracle was on their laps.

Haley giggled and Tessa said, "Stop tilting it! You read what it said."

"Can't help it if I have long legs like a dancer's, can I?" Haley said, tossing her hair over her shoulder. "All right, all right, what do we do now?"

"Put your fingers on one side of the clear circle. It's called a pointer. Now concentrate and keep your dancer's legs still. I'll ask the first question, but it'll be about you."

Tessa's hands were clammy as she put her fingers on the triangle. She closed her eyes. "Dear Great Oracle," she whispered, "tell us. Will Haley meet any great guys at the ranch with her father?"

Haley giggled again and Tessa said, "Sh-h-h. Just keep thinking." She sat, frowning with concentration, her eyes fixed on the pointer. Slowly, almost invisibly, it began to move.

"You're pushing it, Tessa!"

"Am not! Be quiet." The pointer *was* moving, and she had nothing to do with it.

Haley's blue eyes widened as the pointer moved to the left and then back, finally stopping so that the letter *R* showed through the circle. "R?" she said. "What does that mean?"

"Concentrate," Tessa said. "We'll find out."

They waited. At last the pointer moved. It landed on the *R* again. Then it went to the word *Yes* and stopped.

"See?" Tessa shrieked. "Isn't it great?"

"That was easy. There are always lots of guys on a ranch," Haley said.

"But, Haley, don't you see? The two *R*'s! You might be meeting Robert Redford or his son, if he has one. His name's probably Robert too. Remember, he has a ranch out there somewhere."

"Oh, my gosh," Haley said, putting her hands to her cheeks. "Oh, my gosh! Let's do it again. What shall I ask?"

Haley asked when she would marry and the pointer went to the two and four. "Twenty-four!" Haley squealed. "Tessa, it works! It really works!"

"It's because I'm a true believer," Tessa said. And I have the gift, she thought with a shiver of excitement.

"Well, so am I," Haley said. "Go ahead. It's your turn. What are you going to ask?"

"I know exactly." Tessa put her fingers on the triangle. "Dear Great Oracle," she whispered solemnly, "something important is going to happen this summer, and I'm going to make it happen. Tell me what it should be."

When the pointer moved, it circled the board, stopping over the letter *P.* Abruptly, it moved to *A,* then back to *P.* Haley wrinkled up her nose, but her face changed when the pointer moved again. It went to *A* and stopped. They waited for several minutes, but the pointer did not move again.

"Terrific!" Tessa said, disappointed. "Papá, just plain old Papá. What does *that* mean?"

Chapter Five

To Tessa, the next three days were a complete waste. Nothing to do but wait. The boy called Mark had vanished. So had her diary. And so had her hopes of trying a magic spell.

Most of the afternoon of the first day she sat on her front steps, hoping to see the boy return. At dusk she gave up and came in. The next day, just before supper, she decided to try something. It was probably dumb, but she was ready to try *anything* to feel better. With her sister Nita on the other side of the board, she asked the Oracle where Mark was. It did not work. Nita just sat there grinning her little cat grin, pretending that she was trying. When the pointer would not move, she pushed it.

"Nita, stop that! You're doing it all wrong!" Tessa cried. "The pointer moves when the Oracle tells it to." A lot of good saying that did. Nita got up, stuck out her tongue, and left. If only Haley had been home! But Haley had gone to Santa Barbara on Wednesday to visit her grandmother and she would not be back till Monday. So, until Haley came back, the Oracle could not help at all.

Tessa decided that the best thing to do was to keep busy until her neighbor returned. But even keeping busy was hard. For one thing, with Lisa and Haley gone, going to the beach was out. Even though Riggs Beach was just a few blocks away, she was not allowed to go there alone. She might have asked her friend Gail, but Gail, who was as red-haired as Wendell and had the skin to go with it, could not stay at the beach more than five minutes without getting a bunch of blisters. Sure, there was Nita and/or Wendell, but she felt that they were more trouble than company. And just when she might have been glad for more jobs around the house—while she waited for her diary, anyway—Mamá's list of chores had become shorter. Mamá had crossed off window washing and weeding. She did not like the way Nita and Tessa argued about whose side of the glass the spots were on and, no matter how carefully Nana María pointed out the weeds, they managed to pull half a row of new lettuce before they were stopped.

By Saturday Tessa was sure that she would never see Mark or her diary again. Then on Sunday the dark gray sports van rolled up to the Duncan place. Mark and his father—she was sure it was his father—got out and unloaded suitcases and boxes from their car. Half an hour later a moving truck pulled up by the gate and two men in white coveralls began hauling furniture into the house.

All morning Tessa watched Mark and his father coming and going in their big car. She wanted to run out and ask for her diary, but she made herself wait. Better to catch the boy alone. In the afternoon she wandered restlessly around the house. She helped Mamá wash salad greens and then sat on the window seat with a book. But she could not concentrate. Watching television was not possible; Papá was watching a ball game. Nana María's

TV was out, too. In her little house, surrounded by all her pretty potted plants, Nana María was watching a Spanish-language movie. After supper she decided she could not stand around anymore. She *had* to find out what was going on at the Duncan place.

As she hurried across her backyard and the empty lot, she had a horrible thought. What if they had fixed the fence? Once there, she pushed gently against her special boards and relaxed; they were loose. But when she pulled the boards aside and pushed her head and shoulders through the opening, she groaned. The arbor wasn't empty. Mark sat on the stone bench beyond the birdbath, grinning at her.

"So that's how you got in," he said. "I never would've found it."

"Well, now you have," she said crossly. What should she do? She could not just stay there, squeezed between the fence boards.

"Don't just stand there with your head hanging out," the boy said. "Come on in."

She stared at him. He had read her mind. "Okay," she said. "But I want my diary."

"Sure. If I can find it.

"You lost it! I knew you would!"

He shook his head and laughed. "I didn't lose it. I was just kidding. Do you really want it?"

"You bet I do. And right now. I've been waiting for it for days. You just vanished without giving it to me."

"I'm sorry. My cell phone was ringing. I knew it was my dad. When I finally came back, I couldn't find you. I didn't even know your name—unless it's really Athena—

or even where you lived, so . . ." He stretched out his
hands and shrugged. "Besides, I needed time to read it,"
he added with another grin.

"You! You didn't! That's absolutely illegal and . . .
and . . ." She felt her face turning red. "And mean
too. I . . . I personally think you're disgusting."

The boy tossed his head back and laughed. "Jeez, you
fool easy. Just wait. I'll go get your book." He disappeared
around the hedge that enclosed the arbor. When he
returned he had the green book.

She took it from him and held it close. "Thanks," she
said. "I won't lose it again, believe me." Then she added,
"You didn't really read it, did you?"

"Nah. I had better things to do."

Tessa shifted from one foot to the other. Finally, she
said, "Are you all moved in?"

"Just about. We'll camp out in one room while the
workmen finish. When they're done, Dad and I'll start
working 'cause Mrs. Hollis gets here next week."

"Who's she?"

"She's a lady my dad hired to keep house for us."

"Why? Where's your mother?"

"Detroit. She lives there."

I should have known, Tessa thought. "So your folks
are divorced too," she said with what she hoped was cool-
ness.

"Yeah. A year ago. How about yours?"

"Mine? *Mine?* Oh, they're still together." She
shrugged. Except for her parents, just *everybody* was
divorced. She sighed and plopped down on the bench
beside him.

They were quiet for what Tessa figured had to be a year. She could not have thought of so many wrong things to say in less time than that. She shuffled her feet and looked around sadly. This is not my place anymore. I won't be able to come here again. She cleared her throat and said, "I've gotta go."

"Hey, whatever your name is," Mark said, "you can come here any time you want."

Her mouth fell open as she stared at him. "My name's Tessa del Campo," she said, "and you know what you just did . . . *again?* You read my mind."

"I did? How? 'Cause I sure didn't know your name. Mine's Mark Valenti. So how did I read your mind?"

"What you said about my coming here. Don't you believe in that? You know, reading minds, E.S.P., magic?"

"Not really," he said. "But I'll keep an open mind, like my dad says."

She studied him for a moment, then said, "If you promise you won't laugh, I'll tell you something."

"I won't laugh," he said seriously. "And that's a promise."

With slight hesitation, she told him about the Oracle and how it had worked for Haley. Mark did not laugh. He just shrugged and they went on talking about other things.

When they heard a jet above them, he said, "That's what I'm going to be. A pilot. Then an astronaut."

"Fantastic. I'm going to be a writer." She glanced at him. He was nodding seriously so she went on. "Stories just pop out of me all the time. I'll write novels. Of course, I'm going to experience lots of things first. I personally think a writer should."

She did not hear his response because the bells from the corner church began to clang. Seven o'clock. She got up, feeling ill at ease because she wanted to thank him for being so nice about the arbor, but she did not know how to do it.

"I've gotta go," she said again, stepping over his outstretched feet. "Mamá will be looking for me."

"Hey, come back tomorrow. Bring the Oracle if you want."

"Okay," she said, "if you really mean it. I've gotta go," she added for the third time and slipped through the loose fence boards.

In her own room, Tessa sat Raggedy Ann on her diary, spreading the doll's skirt to hide it, then went into the family room by the kitchen.

Her mother looked up from a book. "Well, Tessa, where have you been?"

"Talking to Mark. He's the boy at the Duncan place."

Mamá glanced at Papá, and the look that passed between them was easy for Tessa to read. They hope I have found something, or someone, to help fill my summer. Well, I have, but it's not Mark. It's my magic. A shiver shot up her spine. Tonight's the night!

When it was bedtime, Tessa didn't complain as she usually did, begging to stay up later, arguing that she was almost twelve. Tonight she went eagerly into her room. With the door locked, she turned the pages in her diary to where she had copied "Recipes and Rites for Magic." She read it carefully and then, sighing, she put the book down. Well, this is not a "cloistered covert," but it will have to do. And my nightgown's got to work for a "loose, flowing robe." Anyway, I'm only going to do a little spell, one little one, just for practice.

She dragged her magic things from beneath the bed. She turned off the lamp and pulled open the drapes, letting in the shadowed street light. Now, carefully, she drew a chalk circle on the rug. With the bird feathers, she sprinkled the circle with the rose liquid. It was smelling funny, but she was sure it would work. Next she put the woven crown on her head. With the beaded wand in her hand, she stood in the center of the circle. I'm ready now. I hope I remember everything. She closed her eyes and was about to say the magic words when Nita knocked on the wall between their rooms.

"What'cha doing, Tess?" came her sister's muffled voice.

"Going to bed. What else? Goodnight!" To herself she said, "You won't call me Tess much longer." She took in a deep breath and closed her eyes. Circling the wand above her head, she chanted,

> Magic circle touched with rose,
> All thy power here enclose.

She paused, took another deep breath, then said,

> Spirits, hear my deep desire,
> Keep Nita from calling me Tess.
> Spirits of the air and fire,
> Keep Nita from calling me Tess.

Her eyes half open, so that she would not fall, she whirled around in the center of the circle until she was dizzy. Slowly, she intoned,

> Kiss of wind, race of hare,
> Swirl this message in the air!

There. The ritual was done. The spell was in place. All she had to do now was wait.

Chapter Six

Dear Diary,

It's Monday right after lunch and this is the first chance I've had to tell you the good news. My spell worked! Maybe doing it on a Sunday night helps. Anyway, this morning Mamá really gave it to Nita for calling me Tess. "Your sister's been asking you for months not to do that," she said. "The next time I hear you, Nita I . . . I . . . I'm not sure what I'll do, but it won't be good! Now, remember that."

You should've seen Nita. Eyes as big as Frisbees. Mamá doesn't often talk to her like that. Maybe Mamá was still trying to be nice to me because of the Lisa thing. You're the only one who knows that I really don't care that much. Anyway, I personally and absolutely believe that it was my spell that made her do it today. Of course, Mamá will never know. The magic book made it clear, *and* scary. *The secret spoken, all power is broken.*

Haley isn't coming home today. Her mother (I couldn't call her Betts, no matter if she said I could) told me that Haley is going to stay two more days in Santa Barbara. I sure wish she'd hurry home. And, boy, am I ever glad to have *you* back! Not having someone to tell important things to is bad. Especially for writers. And brand-new witches.

After Tessa finished writing in her diary, she picked up the Oracle and started off for the green arbor. Before she had slipped out of her own back gate, Nita caught up with her.

"I'm going with you, Tes . . .Tessa," she said. "I'm not afraid anymore. Wendell said that Mark said there weren't any ghosts. I think all the hammering must've scared them away. Or maybe they got thrown out with all the other junk. Anyway, I'm going over there with you."

"No, you're not! Besides, dummy, there never were any ghosts. The Duncan place was just an empty house, not a haunted house. I just made that up to scare you. Now, go on home before I put another spell on you."

"What spell? I don't feel anything."

"You will the next time, so go on home!"

But when Tessa started across the empty lot, Nita was still behind her. "Nita," Tessa said in a deep somber voice, "I don't want you following me. Please don't make me use my special magic powers to stop you. I might overdo it because I'm still learning, and if I did, maybe you'd never be able to walk again. You don't want that to happen, do you?"

Nita's black eyes widened as she looked up at her. For a long moment she stared at her sister, her face puckering up as if she was about to cry. Then she took a deep breath and stuck out her tongue. "I think you're crazy," she said, turned on her heels, and ran through the gate into their backyard.

Tessa grinned. Good! She had convinced Nita of her powers. And, besides, what she had told her was true. She did not want to use too many spells until she was really sure of herself. She just might do something bad like . . . like . . . well, like turning a prince into a frog. She was still grinning as she reached the fence. When she stepped through into the arbor, she stopped.

Beyond the birdbath, a narrow red pennant with the word *Go* on it, rose from one of the tall bushes. It moved gently in the rising sea breeze. There was a note dangling from the thin round stick to which the pennant was attached. "Tessa," the note said. "Take my flag down and I'll know you're there. I can see it from the house. After today we'll put it up when you're there. Okay?"

She pulled the note and string off the pennant's pole, and as she did, she thought, he really wants me for a friend. Her grin turned into a happy smile as she slid the flag out of its metal brace. She laid it on the stone bench. When she turned around, Mark was there.

"Isn't that a neat signal flag?" he said.

She nodded. She wanted to say how great it was but her voice was not cooperating. Finally, she said, "It's cool."

Mark rolled the red pennant around the stick and poked it into the ground. "We'll have to find a place to keep it so it won't get wet in case it rains."

"Or real heavy fog. Hey, how about a garbage bag, one of the little ones?"

"Sure," Mark said, "that's what we'll do. And we'll keep it under the bench." He glanced at the birdbath and then back to the bench. "My dad says it's great how you kept this place clean. You must've really scrubbed the birdbath. I told him about the loose fence boards and he said you were smart. He's going to leave them that way. So you can come over any time you like."

"Well," she mumbled. She cleared her throat and finally said, "That's really nice."

"Yeah. My dad's okay." He shoved his hands into his shorts pockets, glanced around again, then said, "Hey, do you want to see the house?"

"You mean it's all fixed?"

"Mostly. Come on. We have to go in the front door. The painters are finishing in the back."

They walked through the overgrown garden and along a path by the side of the house to a long narrow porch that ran across the front. They were stopped before they reached the front door by a shout that came from across the street.

"Young man! You, young man, did you find Homer?" Old Mrs. Herriot leaned dangerously over her porch railing. "Did you hear me?" she called. "Homer. Did you find him?"

Mark and Tessa hurried down the steps to the edge of the street.

"No ma'am," Mark said. "I looked. Honest, I did. No luck, though."

"Tessa, dear," the old lady called in a worried voice, "you've found Homer for me before. Will you look?"

Poor Mrs. Herriot, Tessa thought. That old tomcat's her only company. No wonder she panics. "Okay, Mrs. Herriot, I'll look around."

"I'll go with you," Mark said.

Twenty minutes later they were still looking. "Where could that cat be?" Tessa said as they dragged up the hill. She was hot and sweaty and wishing that she had never gotten mixed up in this.

Mark shrugged. "Maybe if we had some fish or cat food. Maybe he'd come then."

"We should've thought of that earlier." Tessa stopped walking and turned toward him. "Hey, I know what! Let's ask the Oracle where he could be."

"Are you *serious*?"

"Of course I am. It workcd for Halcy."

"She hasn't been to that ranch yet. You won't really know till she goes."

"Oh, it'll absolutely happen. Anyway, let's try the Oracle on Homer."

"It'll be a waste of time," he said, "but okay."

Back in the arbor, she and Mark sat on the bench facing each other, the board on their laps.

"Dear Great Oracle," Tessa whispered, "we have lost a well-beloved cat and a frail old lady is mourning him. Please, please, tell us where he is." She closed her eyes, concentrating, her fingers placed lightly on the triangle. Soon the pointer moved. It went to the letter *H* and then to the *E*. Finally, it stopped on the *R*."

"Her," Mark said. "That's goofy. I don't think this oracle's so great."

"Sure he is. Maybe H-E-R means something else. Maybe it means *here*. Let's look."

Before they were through searching the back garden and the garages, Mark gave up. "I've looked enough," he said. "Besides, the phone's ringing. I'll be right back."

"Okay," she said, waiting eagerly for him to leave because she had another idea. When he had disappeared into the house, she went to the arbor, drew a circle with her toe and stood in the center of it.

"Magic circle touched with rose," she said and stopped. She did not have the rose potion or the wand.

Would this work without them? Of course it would. After all, she was not going to ask for anything *too* world-shaking, just a message to Homer. She started again.

> Magic circle touched with rose,
> All thy powers here enclose.

She paused, took a deep breath and went on.

> Spirits, hear my deep desire,
> Tell Homer I want him.
> Spirits of the air and fire,
> Tell Homer to show himself.

She spun around quickly, raising a dust cloud that started her coughing.

> Kiss of wind, race of hare,
> Swirl this message in the air!

She rubbed out the circle with her foot and started toward the house, scanning the yard for the white cat. When she did not see him, she shrugged and smiled sheepishly. Maybe Mark was right, maybe there was nothing to this magic business. No, no, if she lost her belief in it, of course it would not work. And, besides, maybe the rose potion was terribly important. After all, she had had to wait for it through a full moon. Anyway, where was Mark?

She paused near the back door and called, "Mark!" When there was no answer, she stepped back and glanced at the upstairs windows. She caught her breath. Sitting on a window ledge, looking down on her, was Homer!

He stretched, meowed, jumped to a lower ledge and then to the ground. He padded to her side and rubbed himself against her legs. A chill crawled across Tessa's back and down her arms, turning her skin to gooseflesh. I have special powers and Homer knows it! Cats work with witches sometimes. That's what the pages meant when they said, "A feline is a witch's favored familiar." Homer knows who I am! I know it!

"Mark!" she called loudly. "Mark, come out! I've found him."

Not telling Mark what she had accomplished was hard. Her excitement was ready to spill over. But she reminded herself, *The secret spoken, all power is broken.* And I do not want that. She kept quiet as they delivered the cat to Mrs. Herriot. Then, suddenly, the words spilled out. "See, I told you, Mark, magic really works."

"What magic?"

"The Oracle, of course," she said, proud of her quick thinking. "It told us where he was. What do you think of it now?"

"Lousy speller," Mark said with a grin. "But he made Mrs. Herriot happy."

I made Mrs. Herriot happy! Tessa wanted to shout. But she did not. A real live witch, she told herself, has to remember who she is and act totally mature.

Chapter Seven

Dear Diary,

It's bedtime on Tuesday. Sorry I haven't had time to write before this. I've been spending a lot of time with Mark. This morning I showed him the beach bike path. I was afraid he'd laugh at my clumsy old bike, but he didn't. His is a real racing bike. Expensive. He calls it Lean and Mean. I learned that he likes sports, but then, except for Wendell (who likes nothing but his bike and his computer), what boy doesn't? He says it's too late for baseball, but as soon as his dad and he are all moved in, he'll register for soccer.

Mamá and Papá, and especially Nana María, think Mark is nice. They think he has very good manners. But what's so great about that? Doesn't everybody say "thank you" for a Pepsi?

I finally saw Mark's house. Yesterday, right after we'd found Homer, his father came home, so that wasn't a good time to show it to me. But this morning he did. It's absolutely big. Upstairs there are four bedrooms and three baths and one long room with a row of windows on the west side, so that you can see the ocean and Catalina Island. Well, maybe not Catalina all the time, not if it's foggy. Downstairs they have an absolutely huge kitchen and an even bigger living room, plus other rooms, of course.

I personally think it's too big for just two people. I asked Mark why they needed such a big house and he said they didn't. But he said that the Duncan place was built by a famous architect and his dad, being an architect too, couldn't resist buying it.

Just after dinner tonight, Haley called. She's back from her grandmother's house, and she says she has a surprise for me. Haley, *with a surprise for me?* Awesome!

P. S. I hope you don't mind Raggedy Ann's sitting on you. I'll find a better hiding place soon.

The next day Tessa sat cross-legged on Haley's bed, watching her dig in her suitcase. Haley was kneeling on the floor before it, tossing clothes all over the floor. Finally, she held up a small white box.

"I knew it was here somewhere," she said. "I got black for you because your hair's so entirely dark. I got light brown for me."

"Brown. Black. What're you talking about?"

"Eyelashes. I got us some really glamorous eyelashes. 'Course I had to tell Gram that all the kids here were wearing them." She pushed the suitcase across the floor with her foot and said, "Why are you just sitting there for? Come on, let's put them on."

Tessa watched Haley pull the cover off the white box. On a little square of tissue paper lay the most beautiful spidery lashes she had ever seen. "Are those mine?"

"They're black, aren't they?"

"Oh, Haley, thank you. They're beautiful. But why are they so long?"

"Who cares? I learned all about it. We'll fix them." Haley pulled a chair up to a dressing table and turned on the lights above the mirror. "Sit here. I'll put yours on—they go right over your own lashes—then you can do it me."

Putting the gluey stuff on, wiping it off, and starting all over again took a long time. Finally, Haley said, "Okay, I'm finished. You can look now."

Haley brushed little pieces of the trimmed lashes away from Tessa's cheeks and turned her toward the mirror. Tessa could not believe what she saw. The girl looking back had beautiful black eyes. And she was . . . yes, she was totally pretty! "Oh, Haley, they're fantastic!"

"Sure. What did I tell you?"

They really bring out my eyes, Tessa thought, staring in the mirror. Nana María was right. Hadn't she said I was going to bloom into a lovely girl?

"Hey, stop staring at yourself," Haley said. "It's my turn now."

Haley kept interrupting with orders as Tessa glued the brown lashes on her and trimmed them. But when Tessa was done, Haley said, "That's great. You did a good job." Then they fluttered their lashes at one another and giggled. Later, they walked down to the swimming pool to see if any of Haley's neighbors would notice their beautiful lashes, but nobody did.

"Let's go down to the beach," Haley said. "Gail's going to be there—all covered up, of course—and Jeff and Jenny. Let's see what they say."

"I can't. Mamá said to be back by three. Anyway, I'm dying to show my lashes to them."

Tessa raced home on her bike. The sea breeze was salty and cool as it blew against her face, and she smiled happily. Mamá will love them. She will not believe how pretty they make me look. But when Tessa turned onto Grant Street, she began to have doubts. She pumped up the hill slowly. Maybe Papá will not like them. She shook her head. No, I'm totally wrong. He likes to look at all the pretty girls on TV, doesn't he? So he will like me with my new lashes. Feeling better, she pumped hard and swung eagerly into her driveway.

The house was empty. But in minutes she heard her mother's car in the driveway. Nita ran into the house ahead of Mamá. She stopped dead in her tracks when she saw Tessa.

"Yuck!" she said. "What did you do to your face?"

Mamá came in, a sack of groceries in her arms. "Here," she said, handing the sack to Tessa, "put this on the table." Then she turned and looked again. "Honey," she said, "what's on your eyes?"

"Aren't they super?" Tessa said a little shyly. "Haley got them for us."

Mamá sat down, her shoulder bag slipping down her arm almost to the floor. She ignored it. "I don't know, *mi'jita.* They're not exactly right for you. As a matter of fact . . . as a matter of fact . . ."

"They're yucky!" Nita said, scrambling out of the room.

"As a matter of fact, *mi'jita,*" Mamá said with more determination, "you shouldn't be wearing any makeup, much less fake eyelashes."

"But, Mamá, you haven't even really—" She stopped as the back door slammed and her father walked in.

"Hello, family," he said. "I left the store a bit early." He looked at Tessa and frowned. "What's that on your eyes, Tessa? Fake eyelashes?"

"Yes. Aren't they great? They really make me—"

"They make you look like a floozy," he interrupted.

Tessa cringed and her mother said, "Miguel, please. Be reasonable."

Papá shook his head and his frown deepened. "I'm sorry, Claudia," he said. "I don't want to be unreasonable, but they make her look both cheap and silly. Take those stupid things off immediately, Teresa."

Cheap! Silly! Tessa was not sure she was hearing right. Couldn't he *see?* She felt tears burn eyes and blinked furiously to hold them back. "How can you say that?" she said.

"Don't argue," her father said sharply. "Do as I say!"

"I think you're blind!" she shrieked as she rushed out of the kitchen.

In her room she leaned against the closed door. She took ten deep breaths, trying to calm down, but that did no good at all. The anger chewed away inside of her.

Maybe Mamá and Papá are happy in their practical, dull life, but they do not have to drag me down with them! I cannot go to San Francisco with Lisa! I do not get leather boots like Haley! I cannot have something to make me pretty! I cannot have *anything*! She started to rub her eyes and stopped, remembering the eyelashes. Crossing to the dresser, she flung Raggedy Ann to the floor and grabbed her diary.

> It's unfair!
> Mamá and Papá are absolutely out of step with the rest of the world!

After she slammed the diary shut, she spent the next half hour in the bathroom removing the new lashes. It was not easy. When she was through, she flung herself on her bed and stared at the ceiling, angrier at her parents than she had been before.

They would not even listen. Especially Papá. If it was not for him I could have kept the lashes. Mamá would have softened. Whenever she calls me *mi'jita,* little daughter, I know she's trying not to hurt me. Papá's a dictator, that's what he is. He's the one who has spoiled my whole summer. And he wouldn't even tell Mamá why. I wish I could live with Mamá alone. I suppose Nita would have to live with us too. Well, okay. It would certainly be better than this. She flipped over on her stomach, punched the pillow and mumbled, "Nothing could be worse."

She muttered:

> Spirits, hear my deep desire.
> Let my parents get divorced.
> Spirits of the air and fire,
> Let them get a divorce!

She sat up stiffly. I did not say that, did I? Well, it does not matter if I did. It's not like I did a real spell. I have not done all the other stuff to prepare for it. But, if it gets too bad around here, I *will* do the whole thing! She jumped out of bed and, tearing her door open, stormed out of the house.

Chapter Eight

Tessa scowled as she marched along the side of the house. Peeling off the fake lashes had been messy, and it hurt. To make things worse, she had pulled out some of her own. She stopped as she saw Mark in the center of the street, making wide circles with his bike.

"Hey," he called, "what're you doing?"

"Don't know," she grunted. "Nothing, I guess."

"Is something wrong?"

She shrugged and sat down on the curb. "Don't know."

"D'ya want company?"

"Guess so." Mark threw her a funny look as he got off his bike and sat beside her. Tessa tightened her arms across her chest and muttered, "Guess I'm mad."

"Who're you mad at?"

"My parents," she said, her voice rising. "Who else? All they care about is what *they* think, how *they* feel. Do they ever think of me?"

Mark shifted on the curb. "It's a bummer, isn't it? No fun being caught in the middle like that. I know."

She nodded sadly. "Sometimes I think I'm adopted, but I guess I'm not."

"Yeah. You look a lot like your mom."

"I *do*? She's pretty."

He shrugged. "Maybe you are too."

Tessa stared between her feet at the street. A little rivulet of clear water from their neighbor's garden hose was carrying a dried-up magnolia leaf, like a miniature canoe, along the curb and down the Grant Street hill. Me, pretty? Wait until he sees Haley. My face is too thin, my nose is too long and at eleven and a half, I'm already getting a pimple. Maybe, if they had let me keep the eyelashes . . . She sighed. "Mark," she said, "what's it like to be a divorced kid?"

Mark leaned over and tightened his shoelaces. Then he looked up and said, "I guess it was bad at first. You feel like you're pretty much a nobody. But it gets better. You know, they explain things and tell you they love you and that kind of stuff. It's not all that bad, really."

"That's good," she said and gave the little leaf canoe a shove around a large pebble.

"It's hard to talk about it, isn't it?" Mark said.

"About what?" she said. Then, "Oh. I don't know about that. All I know is that my father's been acting weird for weeks. And that today he was mean and rotten."

"That's too bad. He seems like a nice guy."

"He used to be," Tessa said and got up.

"You want to play a video game with me and Wendell?" Mark asked.

"Uh-uh. I'd better go in now." She walked slowly down the side of the house to the backyard.

Nana María was kneeling by a bed of butter yellow marigolds, weeding. She pushed her big grass hat back on her head and said, "*Bueno, muchacha,* what is that scowl about? And why are your eyes so red?"

"I had to rub hard to get my new eyelashes off, that's why. Papá made me do it." When Nana María nodded solemnly but said nothing, she went on, telling her the whole story. "Nana," she ended, "sometimes I wish I could trade my life for a different one."

Her grandmother sat back, put the trowel and claw with which she had been working down on the ground beside her and said, *"Más vale malo por conocido que bueno por conocer."*

"What does that mean, Nana? Something about bad being better? That's pretty silly, isn't it?"

Nana María smiled. "What it means is that sometimes it's better to keep what one has than to gamble that something new will be better."

"Maybe," Tessa said. "Guess I'd better go in."

"Go," Nana María said, "before I find another *dicho* for you."

Tessa grinned. "Okay, Nana. I guess one of your old Spanish sayings is enough."

Before she fell asleep that night, Tessa thought of something that made her feel better: even though her parents—her father mostly—could keep her from wearing her beautiful eyelashes and otherwise totally ruin her summer, there *was* one thing they could do nothing about. Nothing at all. Because they would never know about it. *The secret spoken, all power is broken.* With that thought held closely, she pulled the fuzzy summer-weight blanket up near her chin, said goodnight to Raggedy Ann and went to sleep.

The next morning Tessa sharpened two new pencils. Then she pulled a sheet of lined paper from her desk. At the top of the sheet she wrote, "Spells To Do." Then she made a list.

- Make something really exciting happen this summer.
- Make me the most popular girl in seventh grade.
- Get the town to build a fun arcade for kids only.
- Make Nita stop shaking up Cokes so she can burp loud.
- Make Wendell grow up!

When she finished the list she brought out her magic things. She drew the circle, sprinkled it with rose potion, and asked the spirits of air and fire for the first thing on her list.

Later, she sat on her front lawn, wondering how long it would take this spell to work. Across the street she saw Homer lying on a chair on Mrs. Herriot's porch. When she called, "Hello, Homer," he opened one eye. He stretched lazily, jumped down from the chair and padded toward her. In the middle of the street he stopped to sniff a grease spot, then he came and sat beside her. She stroked his back and jumped when a spark flew. Another omen! Homer is asking for instructions. What would a witch ask her helper to do? She thought and thought. "Stay close to Mrs. Herriot," she whispered finally. Homer looked up at her and meowed his assent. Then he got up and, without turning back, returned to his chair on Mrs. Herriot's front porch.

The front door of Wendell's house slammed as he bounced out onto the porch. When he saw Tessa he raced

over to her. "Guess what I just did?" he asked breathless-
ly. "I just landed my spaceship on Tamok in the Celasian
Galaxy."

"Big deal," Tessa said sourly. "Don't you have something better to do than play those dumb games?"

Wendell's face turned a hot pink. "That's better than
what you're doing. You're just sitting there."

"I'm not just sitting. I'm thinking, Wendell. Thinking
is the most important part of a writer's work."

"Talk about dumb," Wendell said and left.

She was getting pretty bored waiting for something
exciting to happen when the gate next door clanged. Mark
called, "Hey, Tessa, want to go to Council Park with me?"

"What for?"

"Soccer. I want to register for soccer."

"Sure. Okay. Wait'll I tell Mamá."

When she returned Mark said, "Don't get your bike
yet. I want to show you what Dad got first."

Inside the house Mark said, "It's up here," and they
walked up the newly painted staircase. In the room with
all the western windows, he pointed to a telescope on a
swiveling metal stand. "We got it yesterday. Come on,
take a look."

Mark circled it toward the ocean and showed her how
to use it. It was wonderful! Something like magic. Sail-
boats near the cove seemed only a block away. And a ship
on the horizon seemed close enough to swim to. "I can see
a building on Catalina Island," she cried, "and that's miles
and miles away!" She swung the glass around to Seagate
Point, to the cove, back to Catalina Island, fascinated. The
water seemed close enough to touch.

In a few minutes Mark tugged at her sleeve. "Come on. They'll close the soccer registrations if we don't hurry."

"Okay, okay," she said and reluctantly turned away from the telescope.

Later, on the tree-lined path that wound through Council Park, Mark yelled, "Hey, Tessa, wait!" and stopped his bike. He pointed through the trees. "You've got a lake! I didn't know you had a lake."

"It's not a very big one," Tessa said, "but it does have a couple of swans. If you want, I'll show them to you."

"Cool. Soon as I register."

She waited while Mark went into the recreation building. When he returned they locked their bikes in the rack. She led the way by a sign that said, "Little Lake Trail. No Bicycles or Skateboards Allowed." When they reached a high spot, Tessa pointed across the lake.

"The trail ends on the other side by that white summerhouse."

"Let's go see it."

"There's not much there, but okay," she said. They started walking again.

In a little while the trail became a narrow footpath. They walked single file, Mark in front. When they neared the summerhouse, he stopped. He pointed to a man and women on a bench almost hidden by shrubs that surrounded the summerhouse. He said, "Isn't that . . . isn't that your dad?"

The man had his back to the trail, but there was no question about it. It was Papá. A pretty redheaded woman sat facing him, talking seriously. Tessa was about to yell "Hello," but something, she was not sure what, stopped her.

Mark tugged at her arm. "Come on," he said, "let's go."

She stared at him as he started back down the path and then followed him. There was something in the way he looked that really bothered her. Then it hit her. Holy pajamas! He thinks my father is out with, like *interested in,* another lady. And that's absolutely silly. He and Mamá are . . . he and Mamá just totally belong together. Maybe that lady's a homeless person that Papá is helping. Maybe she was going to drown herself in the lake and he's talking her out of it. Or maybe she's a new saleslady for the store. She could be anybody.

When they got back from the park, Mark hung around her driveway, just straddling his bike. Pretty soon he said, "Sorry we bumped into your dad that way. It sure must make you feel crummy."

"Crummy? Why?"

"Oh, you know. Anyway, she's not as pretty as your mom."

Tessa blushed. She absolutely *hated* to blush! "Wonder what they were talking about," she said quickly.

"Better not ask," he said. "You might not like it."

There he goes again. "Hey, Mark, my father's not . . . you know, he's not . . . he's not . . . he's not unhappy," she finished lamely.

Mark shrugged. "That's good," he said, and swung his bike around. "I've gotta go wash a couple of windows. Mrs. Hollis comes tomorrow."

Tessa was in the kitchen, helping set the table for supper when her father came home. "Hello, Papá," she said, forgetting her vow to ignore him. "I saw you at Council Park today."

A sudden sharp silence filled the kitchen. Tessa stared at Papá. If I had exploded a firecracker right on the table, no one could be acting more surprised. What happened?

Her father put a leather case he was carrying on a chair, opened it, then closed it again. "You did?" he said. "Strange, I didn't see you."

"I know. You had your back to us. I wouldn't have seen you either, but Mark did."

"Mark. I see. Well, some other time," he said, making no sense at all. "What's for dinner?"

"I'll tell you as soon as you tell me what you were doing in the park," Mamá said with a teasing smile. "Playing hooky?"

Papá did not smile back. "Something like that," he said and left the room quickly.

Dinner was everyone's favorite meal: make your own tacos, with Nana María's special spicy shredded beef and Mamá's really special *salsa fresca*. But tonight everyone, except Nana María, who loved to eat, just picked at the wonderful food. Tessa shook her head as she glanced around the table. Something was really weird. Everyone was too quiet. Including Nita, whose favorite exercise was talking.

Later, in her room, Tessa grabbed her diary, ready to write in it, when Nita opened the door.

"Hey, can I come in?"

"You *are* in," Tessa said, shoving the green book under her pillow. "What do you want?"

"Nothing." Nita's voice had a wistful sound. "Nothing, I guess. I'm . . . I'm just looking for something to do."

"Go talk to Mamá or Papá."

"They're busy. Why can't I talk to you?"

"Because I've got some important thinking to do."

"That's what *they* said. Only they didn't say, 'thinking.' They said, 'talking.'"

Tessa bounced up in the bed. "Are they in Papá's little den? With the door closed? And talking?"

"That's what I said, didn't I?"

"What are they talking about?"

"How should I know? I could only hear a little bit."

"Juanita Luz del Campo! You *know* you're not supposed to eavesdrop!"

"I didn't eaves . . . I didn't . . . I didn't do that thing! I was listening. Anyway, all I heard was Mamá laughing."

"Laughing? Why?"

"How should I know? Anyway, maybe I didn't hear right. Maybe she was crying."

"Crying? Oh, Nita, you're probably imagining—" She stopped. What if Nita was right? Slowly, Tessa slid her feet to the floor. "Go away, Nita. I want to do some thinking. Alone."

"What's going on?" Nita said, her eyes filling with tears. "What's wrong with everybody?" She slammed the door hard as she left.

A short while later, Tessa was getting ready to write in her diary once more when her mother knocked and opened the door. "Nita and your father are in the kitchen popping corn," she said. "Do you want some?"

"I . . . I don't think so," Tessa said, looking for signs of tears on her mother's face.

"Why are you staring at me?" her mother said with a puzzled frown. "Is something wrong?"

"I wasn't. Was I?" Tessa felt her face getting hot. "Maybe I was, Mamá. I'm sorry."

Mamá ran a hand over her face. "Well, so long as I look moderately normal, you can stare all you want."

"You look the same as always," Tessa said, and her mother grinned and closed the door.

Chapter Nine

Dear Diary,

Except for the way Papá acted yesterday when I said that I'd seen him at Council Park, and, of course, Mark's totally terrific new telescope, nothing too different has happened in the last two days. I guess the spirits of air and fire could wait all summer to come up with something exciting, so I'd better do that spell over again and set a time limit.

Of course, the spirits might figure that Wendell's showing up at Riggs Beach all slathered with sun screen was exciting. But I didn't. Because, of course, he found me *and* Haley, right away. He put his stuff right next to us and you know him, he stuck like chewing gum. Haley ignored him for a while. Then she got really mean. So Wendell picked up his beach towel and shook it right in our faces. He said, "Shoot, you'd think I had rabies or something," and left. I felt kind of guilty because I didn't ask him to stay, but when he found Mark down near the water I felt better. Haley is really getting stuck up. Lately, all she talks about is getting in with the "right group" in middle school. She says Wendell's hanging around us will spoil our chances. I personally think she's crazy. *What right group?* It's the same old sixth-graders going into seventh.

Something else. It's about my (no, not *my,* and that's what this is about) green arbor. Even though

I'm pretty sure Mark means it when he says I can go there any time, and even though he put out the flag and all, it just doesn't feel the same. I guess it's because the green arbor's not mine any more (not that it ever really was) and, for sure, it's not a secret anymore. Well, as Nana María always says, you can't have everything, and I still have my absolutely best secret, my magic. And it's still a secret because you're the only one who knows.

Did I tell you that it's really gotten HOT? Perfect beach weather. Mamá says I can go down to Riggs Beach again tomorrow.

About two o'clock the next afternoon, it was still hot. Too hot to do anything, Tessa thought as she sat on her front steps. She had not been there long when Mark and his dad drove onto their driveway. Mark jumped out of the car near the front of his house and ran over to her.

"Hey, Tessa," he said in a furtive whisper, "remember the lady we saw with your dad the other day? I just saw her. Dad and I were at the bank, and there she was."

Tessa shrugged. "Really? Well, that's not so strange. Everybody goes to the bank."

"She doesn't just *go* there. She works there. Her name's Mrs. Graham and she's the manager." Mark sat on the step beside her. "My dad went there to arrange for bank accounts and they took him in to see the manager, and there she was."

"So?" Tessa said irritably. "Just shows it was probably business my father and she were talking about the other day."

"Except . . ." Mark picked up a pebble near the steps and threw it across the street. "Except . . ." He bent over, digging in the flower bed for another pebble.

"Except *what*?" Tessa said impatiently.

"Nothing. I'd better go help my dad with the groceries."

"Hey! You were going to tell me something. What was it?"

"Well . . ." He shrugged, took a deep breath and said, "Your father called her while we were there."

"My father? How do you know it was him?"

"For one thing," Mark said, "when the phone buzzed and Mrs. Graham picked it up, the woman's voice at the other end was so loud I heard her say it was Mr. del Campo on line three. And when she answered, Mrs. Graham said, 'Hello, Miguel.'"

Tessa sat up stiffly. "So? That's his name, isn't it? Well, what did he want?"

"I guess . . . I guess he wanted to see her. Because she said, 'The same place?' And then she said, 'All right. The summerhouse in half an hour.'"

Tessa jumped up. "You're imagining it, Mark Valenti! I personally think you're imagining it all."

"I am not!" Mark stood up and faced her angrily. "The only reason I told you was 'cause you made me! Forget the whole thing." Mark started for his gate. Halfway there he turned. "If you weren't so chicken, I'd show you I'm telling the truth."

"I'm not chicken!"

"Okay then, get your bike and we'll go to the park."

She glared at him for an instant, then said, "Wait till I tell Mamá that we're riding to the park." When she returned she said, "I can't be gone too long, so hurry up!"

She swung her bike down the hill without waiting for

him. Mark caught up with her, passed her and then rode alongside her till they reached the park. They put their bikes in the rack and, saying nothing, walked around the lake to the summerhouse. It was empty.

"See," Tessa cried, "they're not there."

Mark muttered, "This is where she said."

"Personally, I don't care what she said. I'm going home." She started to turn on the path, but Mark grabbed her arm.

He jerked his head toward where the trail curved and said, "Hurry! We'd better hide!"

"Why?"

"Just do it!" he whispered and tugged at her arm.

"Don't!" she said, pushing at his hand. "Why?"

Mark tightened his hold on her arm and pulled her toward the shrubbery at the side of the path. "Get down! It's your dad!"

Tessa pushed through the scratchy bushes and fell to her knees. Immediately, she heard voices. One of them was her father's. "These meetings are going to be difficult, you know," he was saying as he came around the bend in the trail. Walking beside him was the redheaded lady.

"What do you mean?" the woman said.

"My daughter stumbled onto us yesterday. Next it will be my wife." He laughed. "After all the care we've taken."

"Would the Point be better?" Mrs. Graham asked as they walked on.

"Good idea," he said. "At least, my kids aren't allowed there."

"Tomorrow at three, then. Now let me ask you something. How will it be if . . ." The words drifted out of Tessa's hearing.

Tessa and Mark waited for a few minutes, and then pushed out of the bushes and brushed themselves. Mark swallowed hard and said, "I'm sorry I was right. Really I am. But no matter if he does like that redheaded lady, that doesn't mean he doesn't love you."

Tessa squared her shoulders. "I *know* that," she said. But she did not know anything really—except that she was scared and all mixed up.

At home she put her bike in the garage and stood in its cool darkness, staring at the gloomy corners, trying to shake away the feeling that nothing was right anymore. Just this morning everything had been okay and now it was not. She needed to talk to someone. But this was something she could not talk to anyone about, not even Nana María.

Dinner that night was hurried because both Mamá and Papá had somewhere to go. Mamá was in charge of a group called Your Community Cares, a bunch of people that helped the homeless, and Papá had to go to the Chamber of Commerce meeting. Tessa was grateful because she could not have avoided looking at Papá much longer. Besides, playing dumb board games with Nana María and Nita made things seem more normal.

When she awakened the next day, the feeling that nothing was right had returned. She had to do something about it. But what? It took her all morning to decide that she was going to ask Mark for a special favor. But by the time she came to that decision, her mother had made other plans for her.

"I'm taking my two girls out to lunch," she said. "Then we'll go to Toby's. They're having a sale on summer clothes."

Tessa said, "Can't we go to Toby's tomorrow?" When Mamá said, no, she said, "Well, can't we eat at home then?" Nita put up such a holler at that that Mamá did not even have to answer, although she gave Tessa a puzzled look. Tessa gave up. Almost.

"Can we do everything fast?" she asked. "I need to be home by two o'clock." This time Mamá gave her an angry look. Tessa stopped talking.

Having lunch and shopping turned out all right after all. She *did* find sandals just like Haley's. It was all right, too, because Mamá did things fast. They were home by two-thirty.

As soon as Tessa could, she knocked on Mark's door. A small dark-haired woman opened it.

"You must be Mrs. Hollis," Tessa said. "I'm Tessa. I live next door. Is Mark home?"

"Indeed I am," the lady said with a big smile. "I'm glad to meet you, Tessa. And indeed he is. Mark!" she called.

Tessa stepped into the big front hall as Mark bounded down the steps. "Hi, Tessa. What do you want?"

She knew exactly what she wanted, but the words came slowly. "I came to ask you if . . ." She stopped to moisten her lips. "Do you think you could . . ." She took a deep breath. "Could I look through your telescope?"

Mark said, "Sure. Why not?"

She followed him up the stairs. Now I'm really spying

on Papá, she thought, but I don't care. And I don't even care that Mark knows.

Mark lowered the telescope stand for her and said, "There. Go ahead."

She circled the glass over the water and stopped at Seagate Point. There were two cars by the stone wall, one that could have been her father's pickup, but she could see no people. "Nobody's there," she muttered. But when she looked through the telescope again, moving it slightly to the left, she saw her father and the redheaded lady standing at the end of the stone wall, almost hidden by a large boulder. As she watched, her father handed a thin black box to the woman beside him.

Mrs. Graham opened the box and smiled. Tessa could read her lips. "It's beautiful," she said and held out the box so they could both look into it. As she did, the sun hit the box and brilliant sparks shot from it.

Diamonds! He's giving her diamonds! Tears blurred Tessa's vision. She dug in her pocket for a tissue and brushed them away. When she focused on them again, Mrs. Graham was walking toward her car. She got into it and, with a wave, drove away. Her father stood at the wall looking out at the ocean for a moment, then he left too. Fighting back more tears, Tessa swung away from the telescope and ran to the door.

"Where you going?" Mark asked.

"Home! Everything's crazy!" She ran down the stairs. Totally crazy. Papá's giving her presents! Outside, she slammed the iron gate so hard that it clanged like a bell. Maybe he can fool Mamá, she told herself, but he's sure not going to fool me.

Chapter Ten

Going to sleep was never a problem for Tessa. Every night she pulled open the drapes so that she could see the stars or the moon, or even the mysterious fog, then put her head on the pillow and, as if she'd flipped a switch, closed her eyes and slept. But not this night. This night she stayed awake at least ten minutes wondering about what she had seen at Seagate Point. Then, when she did fall asleep, she dreamed about it.

In her dream she was a bird that flew to the Point and circled over her father and Mrs. Graham. And when she awakened, the dream was still in her mind. I was trying to keep them apart, she thought, but even as a pesky bird, I sure couldn't do it.

She fought back tears. Papá's going to leave us, and that redheaded lady's going to be my stepmother. I wonder why he likes her? Maybe it's because she has an important job. Not like Mamá. Mamá just stays home. Sure, she helps at the hospital and library and works with Your Community Cares, but none of that is the same as being a manager. Tessa stared at a spot on her bedroom ceiling and frowned. Even so, something's weird. This morning Papá gave Mamá a bear hug and a kiss and said he loved her. So why is he hanging around that Mrs. Graham? Something's really weird.

Tessa tossed in her bed and glared at Raggedy Ann. From her vantage point on the chest of drawers Raggedy Ann stared back, a knowing little smile curving her embroidered lips. With a gasp, Tessa bounced up in bed. Her hands got cold and then they got clammy. Oh, no! *I asked the spirits of air and fire to get my parents divorced. Could that be what's happening?* Then, with a big *whoosh* she let out her breath and shook her head. No, that couldn't be. After all, she hadn't done the whole spell.

She was out of bed and pulling a T-shirt over her head when she thought about Homer. The cold, clammy feelings came back along with the memory. *I found Homer without the magic wand* or *the rose potion,* she thought grimly. *The spirits of air and fire heard me then because I was so awfully sorry for Mrs. Herriott.* She yanked the T-shirt over her head and sat back on the edge of her bed. *The book said you had to be emotionally involved with your request.* She groaned as she pulled on her shorts. *The spirits heard me when I was so mad at Papá too!* My emotions sure *were* involved. *So now he's going to leave us for that lady even though he loves Mamá. And it's all my fault!*

Tessa's arms hung as limply as Raggedy Ann's. *I have made such a mess of everything. I guess I shouldn't have tried spells when I didn't have the whole book. But it doesn't do me any good to think of that now. What I've got to figure out now is* what can I do about it?

After lunch, Tessa wandered around feeling more and more miserable. To add to her misery, the green arbor was not her very own hiding place any more. In the afternoon when she could not stand herself any longer, she hurried out of the house to sit on the front steps. Mark was sitting on the curb so she went and sat by him.

She said, "What'cha doing?"

"Nothing. You?"

She shrugged and kicked at a little pile of leaves that had gathered in the gutter, scattering them near their feet. "Thinking, I guess."

"What about?"

"Nothing. Nothing really."

"Then why bother to think about it?" He pushed at the leaves by his shoe with a little twig and began to whistle softly.

Tessa took a deep breath and said, "Well, if you must know, what I'm thinking about is spells. Do you think people can really put spells on other people?"

"Depends," he said. "What kind of spells?"

"Magic spells. You know, when people do certain things to make other people do certain things."

"Do you mean like voodoo? Like sticking pins in a doll? I saw that in a scary old black-and-white movie once. And the pins really worked. Horrible things happened to the guy the pins were meant for."

"That's what I was afraid of, " Tessa said glumly.

Mark gave her a funny look. "Aw, that was just an old movie," he said. And then, "What do you want to do? Put a hex on someone? Like, maybe, Mrs. Graham?"

"Of course not!" Tessa said huffily. "This has nothing to do with her."

"Sorry," Mark said. "Sorry I brought her up."

They were silent then, each pushing at the leaves in the

gutter, Mark with the twig, Tessa, with her foot. An airplane went by overhead and when it was gone, everything was hushed and quiet. Tessa could even hear the soft creaking sounds of Mrs. Herriott's rocking chair from the porch across the street. Tessa sighed and said, "Well, if someone *did* put a spell on someone and then they . . . they decided that they wanted to undo it, do you suppose they could?"

"Why not?" Mark said with a grin. "All they'd have to do is pull the pins out of the doll."

"Mark! Who's talking about dolls?"

"Well, what *are* you talking about? You're starting to sound creepy."

"I feel creepy, and you're sure no help. I don't know why I told you anything." She jumped up. "Guess I'd better go in."

"Hey, Tessa," he called as she went up the steps, "don't forget to pull *all* the pins out."

That night, when Tessa was going to bed, she tripped on the box that held the Oracle. A sign, she thought. That must mean I'm supposed to ask the Oracle for help. And if it does not mean that, it should not hurt. I need to get help somewhere. So she called Haley.

"I need your help," she said. "Will you come over tomorrow? Or are you going to spend the day at the beach?"

"Yes and no," Haley said. "I'm kind of tired of the beach."

"Then come for lunch," Tessa said. "Mamá likes having you."

"Good," Haley said. "Your fridge is always filled with great stuff."

After lunch the next day, the two girls locked the door to Tessa's bedroom and got the Oracle out. Haley insisted on asking it silly things, and they got some silly answers. For instance, Haley asked what color of nail polish she should wear, and the Oracle got stuck on the letters B and P. Haley giggled and said she was going to paint her nails either black or purple—or maybe both.

Finally, Tessa was able to ask her real question. "How can I undo the thing I started?" she said solemnly, certain the Oracle would know what she meant.

"That's dumb," Haley said. "What thing?"

"I can't tell you. Really. I would if I could."

"Come on, you *have* to tell me," Haley said. "How will I know what to concentrate on?"

Tessa's heart sank. Haley did not give up easily. And she could not tell her about the spell. What could she do to persuade her? "Please, Haley. Just do this one question for me. Then we can go out and look for Mark. Maybe he'll let us look through his telescope."

That did it. Haley promised to really concentrate even though she didn't know what the "thing" was. And she did. But all the Oracle came up with was first the letter *L*, and then the letter *I*. After that the pointer seemed to stop.

Haley flipped her long blonde hair over her shoulder in a new way. "This is stupid. What does that mean?" she said.

"Who knows?" Tessa said, disappointed. Mark's right, she thought, the Oracle's a lousy speller. It never finishes a word. But maybe it intends for me to do a little work, like somehow finishing the word myself.

Later, after Haley was gone, she went to the big dictionary and looked in it for words that began with *li.* She sighed when she saw how many there were, but when, almost immediately, she came to the word *library,* she knew what the Oracle meant. She should have thought of it herself. Maybe she could find *Recipes and Rites for Witchcraft* there, and maybe it would tell how to undo a spell.

Tessa felt guilty when Mamá showed how pleased she was that she wanted to go to the library.

"Yes, yes," she said, "go. But not on your bike. There's too much traffic near the library." And then she added, "Maybe a good book or two will pull you out of the mood you've been in lately." When Tessa started to protest, Mamá said, "Now stop that, *mi'jita.* Whenever I see you sit on the curb, I know there's something on your mind. Please remember," she said, giving her a little squeeze, "you can always talk to me."

Not about this! Tessa wanted to shout. Instead she said, "I know. Okay. See you," and started off for the library.

Tessa walked up the ramp to the big doors at the library and, once she was inside, took a deep breath. Yes, there was that good library smell. She always wondered if it was the books that made it smell that way or if librarians always wore a special perfume.

Pink-cheeked Miss Burnett gave her a nice smile from behind the counter and said a soft hello. But when Tessa asked where she could find a book on spells and magic, she told her to talk to Mrs. Agnew, the reference librarian. Ugh.

Tessa talked to Mrs. Agnew only when she absolutely had to. She was scared of her. Mrs. Agnew had a long, bony face with skinny painted-on eyebrows that moved up and down when she talked just as if they were punctuation marks.

Tessa swallowed hard as she walked up to the reference desk. "I'm looking for a certain book," she said. "It's a book on spells and magic."

"Humph," Mrs. Agnew said, and her eyebrows came close together in a frown. "Magic tricks. It's usually the boys who are interested in that. There are several on the shelves with the party and games books."

"No, no, Mrs. Agnew. Not party tricks. I'm looking for a book called *Recipes and Rites for Witchcraft.*"

Now the eyebrows really moved. They seemed to go all the way to her hairline. She stared at Tessa for a moment and then said, "No, dear, we have nothing like that." She sighed. "But, come along, I'll show you what we do have." She led her to a dark corner against the back wall and pulled a thick book down from the top shelf. It was *A Brief History of Witchcraft.*

Mrs. Agnew frowned as she handed Tessa the book. "I'm not sure this is appropriate for you, young lady," she said. "Perhaps I should call your mother and ask her permission for you to have this."

"Oh, no, Mrs. Agnew! Mamá won't mind." Tessa crossed her fingers behind her back and said quickly, "It's for a special summer project. I . . . I'm studying all sorts of old-fashioned things like . . . like witches and . . . and medicines . . . and . . ."

"Humph. Well, take it. It may not be as bad as some of the books I've seen in the young adult area."

Tessa hurried home, her arms heavy with the book and three young adult novels to show Mamá.

That night she wrote a short note in her diary:

Dear Diary,

   A lot of good my fast thinking—you know, about a summer project—did me. So far the witchcraft book is no help at all. And brief? It's about a million pages long. But I'll just have to keep on reading. I don't know what else to do.

Fourth of July night:

Dear Diary,

   Here I am again. No fireworks at Council Park this year. That's sad. I loved them so much when I was a little kid. Mamá and Papá say the fireworks bring all sorts of people to the park, like pickpockets and guys who like to drink and brawl. So the City Council voted no. I miss having them, but I guess it's all part of growing up.

   Mamá and Papá invited Aunt Lupe and Uncle Jim and Wendell's whole family to supper, though. They even invited Mark and his father. Mr. Valenti said no thank you, but he brought Mamá a little bouquet of flowers and explained that Mark and he were going to do a guy thing over the Fourth. Fishing, I think. Maybe if Mark and his father had been around, it might have been all right. As it was, the whole thing was kind of boring. Okay, the hot dogs and hamburgers and Nana María's enchiladas were super, but not the conversation. All the grown-ups talked about was the Summer Fair.

"The Fair Committee's going all out this year,"
Wendell's father said. "They're putting up a lot of
money for the Seagate Citizen of the Year Award."
Uncle Jim said, "What're they giving away? A
yacht?" And Papá shrugged and said it wouldn't
surprise him if they did.

Wendell was sitting next to me (of course!) and
he nudged me so hard that I almost fell off the
bench. "I hope my dad wins it," he said loudly. And
I said, "That would be nice." But, diary, my heart
sure wasn't in it. The last thing I wanted to hear
about was the Seagate Summer Fair. There's
absolutely only one thing on my mind, and you
know what it is. How can I undo that spell?

Chapter Eleven

After struggling through another couple of chapters of *A Brief History of Witchcraft,* Tessa decided that the librarian was right. This was not a book for "a child" to read. It was long and most of it was boring. It took forever to read the first forty pages. And there was nothing in those pages to help her.

She learned that witches are supposed to have the power to "raise storms, cause crops to fail, and make milk go sour." And what good did that do her? A rainstorm might be useful someday, but sour milk? When she read about love potions and "philters," she shuddered. Now she knew what she had done to Papá. It was more than just the incantations. She had used his aftershave stuff in the rose potion and somehow made him fall in love!

After reading again the names of the chapters, she gave up. Not one single chapter was about removing spells. Anyway, she didn't need to read any more. She had a new idea.

The loose pages she had found in the trunk in Aunt Lupe's attic warned over and over again, *The secret spoken, all power is broken.* So, if she told someone, probably the power of the spell would be gone. I'll tell Mark, she thought. He's a good listener, even though he'll probably say spells have nothing to do with it. He thinks that if divorce could happen in his family, it could happen in anybody's. Well, I know for sure that my spell is doing it in *this* family.

Early the next morning when she saw Mark ride up the hill on his bike, she ran down the porch steps and called to him. "Mark, come here. I've got to tell you something!"

Mark circled his bike and pulled it alongside the curb. He straddled it as he said, "What're you going to tell me? That you pulled all the pins out of the voodoo doll?"

"Cut that out, Mark! I never did put pins in any doll, so there were no pins to—" She stopped as a new thought struck her. How could she have been so dumb? The answer to her problem had been there all the time. She knew now just what she had to do. "See you later, Mark," she called and turned back toward the house.

"Hey, what did you want to tell me?"

"Nothing," she called as she pulled open her screen door. "Anyway, I've changed my mind."

"What did I say?" Mark yelled. "Hey! I said it was just a dumb old movie."

For the rest of the day, Tessa struggled with her new plan. When she was called to dinner, she gathered up papers piled on her desk and scattered over the floor, hiding them deep in a drawer.

There were two desserts that night. Mamá smiled as she brought a carrot cake and a lemon pie to the table. "I want you to vote," she said. "Which shall I bake for the fair?"

Papá ate a serving of each and said, "It's a hard decision, Claudia. Maybe you should give us a few more choices."

"Where would I find the time?" she said. "The fair's only a week away."

"That's too bad, eh, kids?" Papá said with a wink.

Tessa stared at him. How can he act like nothing's wrong? She was starting to get mad at him when she remembered. He cannot help it. He's under a spell. And if I do not do something soon, terrible things will happen. She jumped up. "Can I be excused?"

Back in her room she dragged out her papers, sharpened pencils and stared at her desk. What, she asked herself, is the opposite of a circle? Of a long, flowing robe? What's the opposite of above my head? And if the rose potion's wet, then . . . She reached for paper and pencil. I'll write the words backwards too.

A frown deepened on her forehead as she crossed out a line here, a few words there, then crumpled up the paper and started all over again. Finally, she sat back.

"Maybe this will work," she muttered, reading what she had written. When she reached the last two lines, she thought, the backwards words are the hardest. I'd better learn them first.

> Ssik fo dniw, ecar fo erah,
> Lriws siht egassem ni eht ria!

Slowly she said the words. Over and over she whispered them until she had them memorized. It was almost bedtime before she was ready to begin. At the living room door she called good night to her parents.

"Going to bed already?" Mamá asked. "Are you feeling all right?"

"I'm fine. I've been writing. There's . . . there's something I want to finish."

Mamá said, "Good night, then," and Tessa left.

From the bathroom she took a container of talcum powder into her room. Quickly, she put on her shortest and tightest white shorts and a tank top. This certainly isn't long and flowing, she thought. It's got to be right. Now came the hard part. Waiting. Waiting until Papá locked the house and he and Mamá went to bed. She sat on the edge of her desk chair, impatient to begin. At last, she heard her father checking the outside doors and the closing of their bedroom door.

Then, as she had done with her first spell, she knelt on the floor with a piece of chalk. This time she drew a square. Carefully, she powdered the outline with talcum. The opposite of rose potion, she told herself as she shook the talcum out, has to be something dry.

Ha-a-a-choo! She sneezed, blurring some of her outline. The rest of the sneezes (she counted, there were eight) she muffled in her pillow. Once she was sure that the sneezing was over, she took the jeweled wand and placed it in the center of the square. Now she was ready. She closed her eyes, stood perfectly still and whispered,

> Magic outline, dry and square,
> Let your power be strong and fair.

She paused, then went on.

> Spirits, hear my deep desire,
> Undo the thing I asked for last.
> Spirits of the air and fire,
> Undo the whole divorce thing fast!

She stepped on the wand, keeping it below her toes. The other time she had raised it above her head. With arms held stiffly at her sides, she chanted,

Ssik fo dniw, ecar fo erah,
Lriws siht egassem ni eht ria!

Then, because she wanted to be sure the spirits had heard her, she repeated the backwards chant. As she finished, a patch of light fell on her. Nita stood in the open doorway, the hall light behind her.

"Hey, Tess," she said, rubbing her eyes. "I've been hearing funny noises. Have you? What's all that white stuff on the floor?"

"Nothing. I spilled something. I'm cleaning it up. Go back to bed."

She closed the door after Nita as quietly as she could. On her knees, brushing the talcum into the rug, she thought, I did everything as opposite as I could. Maybe it will work. Suddenly, she stiffened and put down the brush. *Maybe it has!* Nita just called me "Tess" again, didn't she?

The first thing Tessa thought of when she awakened the next day was the backwards spell. She was very pleased with herself. She was certain that doing it backwards would undo the spell she had put on her father. As sure as she was, though, she wanted something to tell her that it was working. When the phone rang and it was Papá, she hoped that this would be the something she was waiting for.

Mamá listened for a while, before she said, "*¿Qué es esto, Miguel?* What is this?" She nodded, then added, "Look, when I know I'll tell you right away. But why do you need to know where I'm going to be when? No, Miguel, I'm not upset. Just wondering what you're up to. You've been acting so strange lately."

Tessa's heart sank all the way to the floor. No, this was *not* the something she had hoped for. On the contrary. Later, when she went into the kitchen, she found her mother splashing paint on poster paper, making signs for the bake booth. Mamá put the paint brush down. "That father of yours, Tessa," she said, shaking her head, "what in heaven's name has come over him?"

Tessa's mouth dropped open. She looked around the room and then out the window. A bird was hopping from branch to branch in the jacaranda tree. She watched him until he flew away, then stared at her feet. Mamá's words were loud in her mind. . . . *what's come over him?* Tessa rushed out of the kitchen without answering. She was afraid she was going to cry. In her room she pushed Raggedy Ann aside and grabbed her diary.

> Here I am, diary, g-r-r-r! That is how totally not happy I am. What I am is totally miserable. The backwards spell is a bummer. When I think of all the work that went into it, I . . .I . . . well, I want to shriek and pull my hair out, neither of which makes any sense to do. Good-bye!

That afternoon when Aunt Lupe came over, Tessa felt even worse. Aunt Lupe did not stay long, just long enough for a glass of iced tea with Mamá out by the jacaranda tree. Tessa was not sure whether or not they had gone out-side to talk, but, in any case, the kitchen window was wide open and she happened to be standing right there, so she heard all they said. It was all about Papá.

"What's going on with Miguel?" Aunt Lupe asked. "He's been acting so funny lately. Not at all like the brother I'm used to."

"I know," Mamá said somberly. "Not at all like the husband I'm used to either. I tell you, Lupe, it's beginning to worry me."

"Try not to worry," Aunt Lupe answered. "I'll squeeze the reason out of him. He never could keep a secret from his big sister."

Tessa cringed and moved away from the kitchen window. Everybody's starting to notice what Papá's doing. And I'm not helping him. The backwards spell is not working. It was a dumb idea, anyway. And even if it was going work in a day or two, I cannot wait. Everybody will know about Papá by then. I've got to do something *now!* The only thing now is to tell someone what I did. *The secret spoken, all power is broken.* And that is what I need now, to break the powerful spell. It will be sad not to be a witch anymore, but—she took a deep breath and straightened her shoulders—I *have* to do it. I made a bad mistake and—a long sigh—I'm gonna have to pay for it.

Maybe the best person to tell is our Youth Jam counselor. After all, he's a minister even if he does not let us call him anything but Roy. And being a minister means that he *has* to keep what I tell him a secret. Right. No sooner was that thought complete than another dreadful one came barreling into her mind: *They used to burn witches, didn't they?* She sank slowly on to a kitchen chair. I'd better not tell anyone who might let that happen, she thought, because what if they still do? No, no, there has to be a law against it. But what if, for some weird reason, they can? It would be totally terrible. No way could she take that chance. Besides, Mamá and Papá would really miss her.

Of course, there was Haley. But Haley would not recognize a secret if it came up and bit her. Tessa looked out the kitchen window at Nana María's little house. Right in her own backyard was the best secret keeper in the world. A while later, after Aunt Lupe had gone, Tessa went out into the garden.

She found Nana María pinching the old blooms off the rose bushes. "Can I help you, Nana?" she asked.

"Of course. Just watch out for the thorns."

They worked silently for a moment. It was late afternoon and there was a pleasant little sea breeze to cool down the sun. The roses, old and new, were beautiful and smelled so pretty that Tessa found it hard to believe that on a nice day like this she could be in so much trouble. She sighed, a long, sad sigh, and Nana María turned quickly to look at her.

Tessa said, "Nana, did you ever know any witches?"

"Witches, eh? *Brujas.* So that's what you're thinking about." She smiled. "I certainly did. Several of them. What mouths they had. Never had a kind word for anyone."

"Not mean old ladies, Nana. I mean real *brujas.* The kind that can put spells on people."

Nana María nodded, got up and went to the small bench by the lemon tree. Tessa sat down by her. Her grandmother said, "Oh, yes, I've known one or two of those too. There was an old *curandera*—an old woman of many medicines—in the village where I lived until I married. She worked many spells."

"How? Did she put pins in dolls?"

"No, no, that was not her way. Mostly, she brewed herbs and other things—"

"To drink?"

"Sometimes. Sometimes the teas she brewed were used as lotions or to spread on places to drive away evil. Some were used to attract people." She grinned a shy little grin. "I used a special brew to attract your grandfather. I rubbed it on the outside of a glass in which I gave him lemonade, and once the potion got on his hands I knew that he was mine."

Tessa looked wide-eyed at her grandmother. "Did it work?"

"He married me, didn't he?"

"But would he have married you even without the potion on the glass?"

"Of course, Teresita. Those were just fun things for the boy-crazy girls of my village to do, things for us to whisper and giggle about."

"So you don't think spells or magic potions really work. I mean good *and* bad ones."

"Who knows? But if there *are* spells, the only thing that can cancel them is one simple little word. Can you guess what that is?"

Tessa was too excited to think clearly. Could it be possible? Sure, everybody knew that her grandmother had a green thumb and all that, but was it possible that *Nana María knew how to break a spell?* "No, Nana," she said, "I can't guess."

"Truth," Nana María said seriously. "Spells and bad magic can never work if they are challenged by truth."

Tessa frowned. She was back to square one, right where she had started. "You mean if the witch tells someone the truth about what she did?"

"Not just someone. No, that wouldn't work. The truth must be told to someone who was touched, no matter how, by the spell."

Chapter Twelve

Tessa nodded, said good-bye to Nana María and hurried into her room. Once the door was closed, she stretched out on the bed and groaned. Okay. So that meant that she had to tell the truth to her father or mother or—ugh!—Mrs. Graham. But why did it have to be one of them?

It wasn't that she didn't trust Nana María. She totally did. After all, *The secret spoken, all power is broken* said practically the same thing as telling the truth. It was just that telling one of *them* the truth was going to be seriously hard to do. Like telling Papá. She couldn't do that. Not after the eyelash thing. Mamá was the best one. And there was no use in waiting. She'd better do it right now.

Tessa slid off the bed and at the same instant heard the piano being played. There went her do-it-now good intentions. First, because everybody knew that Mamá was not to be interrupted at the piano unless it was a terrible emergency, like "Nita broke her leg," or "The stove's on fire." Second, because Mamá was playing Debussy's "Clair de Lune," a nice, soft piece, and that meant that she was stressed out and was trying to calm down and did not need more trouble. So telling her the truth would definitely have to wait.

Tessa sighed and went into the kitchen. Except for Mamá's music, the house was quiet, which meant that Nita was gone, probably down the street playing with her friend Winnie Wong. At the refrigerator, Tessa poured herself a glass of lemonade and was about to turn on the kitchen TV when she saw the big yellow circle on the family bulletin board. A yellow circle meant a message for her. Red circles were for Nita; green, for Papá; white, for Mamá. Nana María's messages were all hand-delivered. Tessa pulled down the yellow circle and read, "You have an e-mail message from Lisa—but set the table for supper first."

At bedtime that same night, with Raggedy Ann sprawled on the pillow beside her, Tessa wrote:

Dear Diary,

My good intentions flew out the window. The ones about telling Mamá the truth right away. Because after supper the house was jammed full of Seagate Fair people with all their last-minute plans. The fair starts day after tomorrow, remember.

As for Lisa's e-mail. Did I get chance to read it then? No. I barely got a chance to read it after supper. The Seagate Fair people had dibs on the computer too. They're out there now, walking back and forth from the den to the living room. Like Mamá said, it was Papá's and her turn to have the meeting, but why did they have to invite so many people? Besides, they all think Nita is adorable! Ugh! But back to Lisa's e-mail. It wasn't all that interesting. More like weird.

She said San Francisco's the greatest, but that the girls at camp are such snobs. She can't believe how annoying they can be. She said her dad was gone to Japan the first week she was there, which meant she was really visiting her stepmother and Matthew, her baby half-brother. I don't think she liked that part of it.

At the very end she asked about our gang. She asked about each one separately. How do I know what they're all doing? I've been busy myself. Wait till I tell her about my new friend Mark. She wanted to know, too, how the waves were at Riggs Beach, and asked if I go down there every day. And you won't believe this, she said she wished she could be here for the Seagate Summer Fair. Holy pajamas! The fair! Do you suppose she's not having that much fun?

That's all for now, diary. I'd better get plenty of sleep. Because tomorrow I have to tell Mamá the truth, and who knows what'll happen then!

What happened the next day was that there was no time to talk to Mamá about anything that needed more than two sentences. And for sure not something that would take Mamá's attention away from what she was doing. The warm, sweet, yummy smell that filled the house would tell anyone that Mamá was baking up a last-minute storm. Two more pans of brownies (made from scratch, of course) to be cut into single serving squares were in the oven. Another layered carrot cake with cream cheese frosting in between the layers was on the kitchen table. A couple of loaves of orange-nut bread that made Tessa's mouth water (there was nothing better than a slice of this with lots of butter) were in progress, along with a double recipe of lemon bars. Tessa had made her mind up before breakfast that there would be no time for telling "the truth" today.

Nor was there time on the following day. Tessa, who was caught up in all the prefair activities—chopping walnuts and washing up baking pans on one day, helping to decorate booths on the next—gave up. She would have to wait until after the fair to talk to Mamá.

Ten minutes to six on Saturday, the fair booths, which were scattered throughout Seagate High's football field, were practically ready. The red, white, and blue bunting around the presentation platform required only a few more nails to hold it firmly in place; the night lights and the public address system had stopped blinking and sounding and were declared ready; and, at the chili dog concession, dozens of fat, pink wieners were lined up, ready to be tossed into a steamer.

At exactly six o'clock, the mayor, a round little man with a round bald head, cut a ribbon at the entrance to the football field. He also bought the first ticket to the Gallery of Ghastlies. But he was not going to be the first to go through the Gallery. While he and other fair officials made introductions and announcements from the presentation platform, the young crowd had lined up at a big tent near the end of the football field that held the Gallery of Ghastlies.

Tessa and Haley found themselves near the center of the long line, four or five people behind Mark and Wendell. Not far behind them were Jenny and Gail. When the Gallery opened, Tessa and Haley handed their tickets to a white-faced, sharp-toothed Count Dracula and walked into a hallway lined with heavy curtains. Pale lights hid behind red paper, filling the place with an eerie pink light. A paper skeleton dangled at the end of the hallway. From a closed coffin came moans and groans.

"It's like Disneyland at Halloween," Tessa whispered. "This is fun."

"Whatever," Haley answered with a shrug. "There's nothing scary here."

Huddled together, the girls turned a corner into a darker hallway. They took a few hesitant steps. Suddenly, from behind a curtain, two bodies hurled themselves at them. Haley shrieked. Tessa squealed. And behind them Gail and Jenny screamed and giggled.

Haley was standing absolutely still, her hand at her throat, when Tessa saw four familiar feet below the curtains. She giggled. "It's all right. It's only Mark and Wendell."

"Wendell?" Haley said sullenly. "That dork? He wouldn't have the nerve."

"Stop it, Haley! Wendell's all right. I personally think you're mad because he scared you. In fact, Mark and Wendell are scaring everybody. Listen to the screaming."

The shrieks and squeals had gone down the line all the way to the entrance. The girls looked at each other and started laughing. When they reached the exit, Gail and Jenny said they were going through the Gallery again. Haley said, no, she was hungry.

"Come on," she said and pulled Tessa toward the hot dog stand. The rich, spicy smell of steaming wieners made Tessa's mouth water. When Haley ordered a chili dog, she did too. They climbed up to the highest row at one end of the bleachers to eat them.

Tessa had taken only one bite when Haley cried, "Oh, shoot the moon! Look what I've done! I've splattered chili all over my white shorts!"

"That's awful," Tessa said. "But it'll wash out, won't it?"

"Not tonight, it won't, and I can't go around like this. I'll just have to get a ride home and change."

"Now? Finish eating first."

"No way," Haley said, starting down the bleachers. "Who wants the dumb old thing."

"I want mine," Tessa said and watched Haley pick her way through the crowd. Tessa continued to sit at the bleachers. She ate her chili dog slowly. It surprised her, but she had to admit it. She was having fun. Maybe the idea of a hometown fair was not all that bad. It was just that earlier in the summer she had had so many exciting things planned to do, like going to camp with Lisa, like turning her secret green arbor into a witch's circle, and like learning to produce some magic spells. It had been an exciting summer to look forward to and then the bottom had totally fallen out of all her plans—except for the magic spells. She had learned she could make *them* work, all right. Look at the mess she was in.

Tessa squirmed uncomfortably on the rough wooden bleacher. I will not think of that right now, she told herself. So far everything here has been fun. I even enjoyed looking at the Chamber of Commerce display booths. The one with the pictures showing Main Street one hundred years ago all the way till now is super. Even the bake booth is better than I expected. Maybe calling it the Cookie Jar is not all that great, but wearing old-fashioned clothes and selling old-time cookbooks is a pretty good idea. Wonder if it was Mamá's?

As Tessa took her last bite, she saw her mother by the Cookie Jar. In her long skirt and ruffled blouse, Mamá looks awfully pretty, she thought. Much prettier than that Mrs. Graham.

Just then Tessa gasped. She had caught sight of a familiar redhead below her in the first row.

Mrs. Graham! Oh, no! I must've called her up. I absolutely *am* a witch! And to make things worse, there's Papá looking for her. Something's still pulling him to her. If only I could have told Mamá the truth, maybe the dumb spell would be over.

Her father came out of the crowd and walked toward the bleachers. Tessa crossed her fingers, hoping he was looking for her. But no such luck. It was Mrs. Graham he came to sit beside. They talked, their heads close together. In a moment he stood up, glanced around him carefully, and hurriedly walked away.

She sat feeling helpless and alone, her eyes on the red head below her. As she watched, Mrs. Graham took a mirror from her purse, rubbed on lipstick and ran a comb through her hair. Tessa groaned because suddenly she knew what she had to do. She had to undo the spell right now. When Mrs. Graham rose and walked around the end of the bleachers, Tessa shot up and went hurtling down the rows after her.

It was darker away from the field. The lights were blocked both by the tent and the bleachers, but Tessa could still see Mrs. Graham. She had stopped and was holding on to the frame of the bleachers, shaking something out of her shoe.

"Hey, Mrs. Graham!" Tessa called. "Mrs. Graham, you have to stay away from my father!"

"*What?*" The woman put on her shoe and turned to face her. "Your father? What are you talking about?"

"About . . . about . . . that you shouldn't be seeing him," Tessa said.

"What's all this? Who are you?"

Tessa fought back tears. "Please, Mrs. Graham, you've got to help me."

"Help you? How? What's the problem?"

The words tumbled out of Tessa's mouth. "My father really doesn't love you. I mean, not really. You may think it's for real, but it isn't that at all. I can tell you what's—"

"Stop it, young lady! You're not making any sense. I think you must have the wrong person." Mrs. Graham turned to leave.

"Don't go!" Tessa's voice was shrill. Mrs. Graham stopped and Tessa went on. "You've gotta stop seeing him, I tell you! You don't understand! You're the one I have to tell the truth to. You're the best chance I have!"

"What do you mean, the best chance?" She stared at Tessa for a moment and then shook her head and smiled. "Oh, I get it now. It's a game you're playing. You're on a dare."

"No, no, I'm not!"

"That's all right. I understand. You're not allowed to explain yourself. Is it like a treasure hunt? Do I have to give you something, a token of some sort?"

"Margaret!" A man's voice called from the darkness at the rear of the bleachers. "What's holding you up?"

"Coming, Cal," Mrs. Graham called. Then to Tessa, "All right, I've heard enough. Here, take my business card. That should prove to your friends that you talked to me. And, by the way, you really had me going for a minute." She pressed a card into Tessa's hand, and turned and walked briskly away.

Late Saturday night, Tessa wrote in her diary.

> I'm only going to write a little bit, diary, because
> I'm completely pooped. Nita and I had to help
> Mamá and Papá store all the baked stuff for tomor-
> row in the school cafeteria and that took a long time.
> Sure, the other ladies helped, but they're not like my
> mother; she can go on forever. Nita complained.
> She wanted to run around with her friends, but I
> didn't care. I sure wasn't having fun anymore. Not
> since talking with Mrs. Graham.
>   "When she walked away I just stood there, feeling
> more stupid than I have ever felt in my life—and
> angrier! *She didn't believe me!* I wanted to yell some-
> thing mean, but I didn't. I got a stomachache
> instead. I could blame the chili dog, except that I'm
> practically sure I'm getting an ulcer. All this worry.
> Tomorrow I'm asking the Oracle for help. Not that I
> don't trust Nana María. I totally do. But I've already
> tried telling "the truth" once—for all the good it did.
> Personally, I think it never hurts to use everything
> you've got. I'm sure you'll agree. Good night.

The next morning Tessa went to the green arbor, took
down the signal flag and waited for Mark. When he finally showed up, she said, "Mark, I've gotta tell somebody
about everything that's been happening. Can I tell you?"

"More magic stuff? I guess I can stand it. Go ahead."

Tessa took a deep breath, swallowed hard and told him
how she'd found the pages, prepared the rose potion, and
how, without meaning to, she'd put a spell on her father.
Mark listened without laughing but when she was
through, he said, "You didn't do anything, Tessa. The
trouble with you is that you have a wild imagination."

"I know. My mother says it's my imagination that will
make me a good writer. But, even if you don't believe it,

I know what I did. And I need your help. I want to ask the Oracle what to do next."

Mark shrugged, let out a long deep breath, and said, "All right, all right, but don't expect me to believe it."

They sat on the stone bench, with the board on their knees. The Oracle was stubborn. The pointer refused to move. "It's your fault," Tessa said. "You're not taking this seriously."

"How can I take any of this seriously. Undoing a spell? I think you're flipping out. You don't have any more magic powers than I do! And I don't have any!"

Tessa bit her lip. "Please, Mark, please concentrate. I told you my secret, didn't I? And that was absolutely forbidden. So the least you can do is help me."

Mark rolled his eyes toward the sky above the arbor. "Okay," he said with a shrug, "ask it again."

"Dear Great Oracle," Tessa said, "I tried to tell the truth to Mrs. Graham, and that didn't work. So I've come to you. Please tell me. How can I undo the spell I put on my father?" They held their fingers lightly on the pointer and waited. At last, it moved, going to the letter *M*. "Please, Oracle," Tessa begged, "please tell us more."

The pointer went directly to the letter *A*. Then it circled the board, landing on the *M* once again. It paused there then returned to the *A,* where it stayed unmoving.

"You've spelled 'Mamá,' Oracle," Tessa said with a long sigh. "All right. I know what you mean. I've got to tell Mamá the truth. Nana María told me that too. All right. That's what I'll do."

"What're you mumbling about?" Mark asked. When she shrugged, he added, "I'll bet all the time you were thinking about your mom and your fingers did what you were thinking. That must be how this board works."

She nodded, blinking back tears. "I was thinking how she'll hate me when she finds out the truth. Last night I thought if I told Mrs. Graham, Mamá wouldn't ever have to know what I'd done. But I've got to tell her."

"If your dad doesn't tell her, I guess you have to," Mark said somberly. "What a bummer."

Tessa nodded. "I know. I'll tell her the whole thing. But right after the fair."

Chapter Thirteen

When Tessa came into her yard, she found Nita sitting on the back porch steps. Nita's eyes were dark and stormy.

"You look weird," she said to Tessa. "What's wrong with everybody?"

Tessa was already feeling bad, but one glance at Nita and she felt even worse. She put the Oracle down and sat beside her sister. It was almost noon, and the sun beat down on the top of her head. Any other time she would have enjoyed the hot, melty feeling, but she could not today. Nita is miserable, she thought. I had forgotten all about her, but she's caught right in the middle of this mess too.

Nita nudged her. "Hey, Tess, I asked you something. Why's everybody acting so weird? 'Specially you and Papá. The only one around here who's okay is Nana María."

"Nothing wrong with me," Tessa said. "I'm just awful busy. But Papá . . . well, he's picky because he has something on his mind."

"What?"

"It's something he's doing, something he doesn't really want to do."

"Well, why does he? He doesn't have to. He's a grown-up."

"Sometimes," Tessa said, feeling at least a hundred years old, "sometimes grown-ups have to do what they don't really want to."

"Why?"

Tessa frowned. "With Papá it's because he can't help himself," she said, picking up the Oracle. "And it looks like nobody else can help him either," she muttered and slammed the door as she went into the house.

Tessa was sure that Mamá would be in the kitchen baking again. But she was wrong. Mamá was at the piano, playing her favorite piano concerto, the soft, slow part that always made Tessa want to cry. Especially today. She leaned against the wall in the hall and listened.

Maybe Mamá and Papá are not perfect, she thought. Maybe they do not do exciting things or have exciting jobs. No one would say owning a hardware store is totally glamorous. It's not the kind of job that takes Papá flying all over the world like Lisa's father or Haley's mom. But I like that. I like having them around. And now, because of me, maybe Papá will not be around anymore. Tears pushed into her eyes. Guess I'm not much of a prize as a daughter.

"Tessa." Her mother was at the door.

Tessa felt a tear run down the side of her nose. Quickly, she brushed it away.

"Why are you just standing there?" her mother asked. "Are you all right?"

"Sure. I was just listening."

"I guess there's no law against that," her mother said with a smile. And then, "About tonight, Tessa. Wear your new shorts and a good shirt, will you?"

"Why? I might ruin them."

"I know. But your father's getting fussy about how you and Nita dress. Try to be as neat as Haley."

"Me? Like Haley? You've gotta be kidding." Tessa tried to sound normal, but her thoughts almost spilled over. Papá wants us to look special for *her.* How *dare* he? Almost immediately, she felt guilty. Of course. He could not help it. "Mamá," she said. "About Papá. I know he's been acting funny lately and there's something—"

"Funny?" her mother said. "More like very, very strange. But Nana María swears he'll be over it in a day or so. So just relax and enjoy yourself. That's what I'm going to try to do."

"Sure, okay. But right now, *please,* Mamá, I need to tell you something."

"Can it wait, *mi'jita*? I'm being pulled ten different ways. In fact, right now I need you to go help Nana María with lunch. Your father will be home soon and I have to leave this minute to get the Cookie Jar ready. The fair opens again at two, remember?"

"When *can* we talk? We really have to."

Her mother gave her a searching look. "It sounds important, but can it wait till tonight? Right after the fair?"

"I guess. But you'll be tired and it'll be late."

"That's all right. If it's that important to you, we'll talk."

Right after Tessa's mother left, carrying more paper stuff for the Cookie Jar, Papá called. He was helping repair a couple of booths at the fair and wouldn't be home till just before supper.

Nita had a yelling fit. "Winnie Wong is going at three!

Why can't we go then too?" Nana María gave her a look and said quietly that they would go when Papá took them, and Nita stamped off to her room and sulked for five minutes.

That evening, after an early supper, Tessa dressed in her new white shorts and a cotton print shirt. This better be good enough, she thought as she walked toward the den. When she stepped through the door, her father put down the newspaper he had been reading. He threw her a glance and stood up.

"You look nice, Tessa. I'm glad you changed because tonight's important."

"Why? What's so special about tonight?"

"Can you keep a secret?" he asked.

"I guess," she answered. But she wasn't sure she wanted to hear what he had to say.

"This secret is something that concerns all of us," he said. "Your mother will know about it tonight before the fair is over."

"Why are you telling me first?"

"Your Aunt Lupe suggested it. She thought you and Nita shouldn't be taken by surprise."

"Aunt Lupe? She *knows*?"

"She wormed it out of me. And I have to say it was a relief to tell someone."

"Well I, personally, don't want to hear it," Tessa said, taking a step toward the door. "I can't believe you're planning to tell Nita too."

"Of course I am. She needs to know."

"I can't believe you!" Tessa said angrily. Spell or no spell, this was too much! After all, she had not asked the spirits of wind and fire to make him lose his common sense. *Tell Nita before he told Mamá?* That was like unbelievably mean. She swung around to leave and bumped into Nita. Her sister was wearing a frilly pink dress and white Mary Jane shoes. "Does Nita have to wear *that?*" she fumed. "She looks like cotton candy with shoes on."

"Leave her alone," Papá said quickly, patting Nita's head. "She looks lovely."

It was close to seven when they reached the park. The football field was crowded with people. Most of them were milling around the booths. A few were sitting on the bleachers. There was a line at the Gallery of Ghastlies and another at the Cookie Jar. They left Nana María at a booth where two of her church friends, Señora Aguilar and Mrs. Reilly, were selling tea towels, pot holders, and colorful candles. They saw Uncle Jim in his wheelchair and Aunt Lupe by his side. They were both eating hot dogs. Papá called a quick hello and walked right by them. Tessa saw Gail and Jenny racing after a balloon that was sailing high above their heads. They caught the string and held on tight.

When Tessa saw Mark and Haley by the popcorn booth, she said, "See you later, Papá. There's Haley."

"Hold it, Tessa. You can't go yet. There's someone I want you to meet."

"Me, too?" Nita said hopefully.

"Both of you," Papá said. "Come along."

Tessa went along. That was not easy because something inside of her was pulling her back. But there was no way out of it. Nita, beaming with pride in her pink frills, bounced happily beside Papá. They went alongside the bleachers toward the gym.

A voice from behind them called, "Miguel! Miguel! Wait up!"

They stopped and turned. Mrs. Graham, her red hair bouncing prettily around her face, was running toward them. "I was afraid you'd never get here," she said. "Can we talk alone?" Her glance fell on Tessa and she frowned. "Aren't you . . .?" She tilted her head and studied Tessa's face. "Yes, of course, you are. You're the funny girl from last night."

A blush burned Tessa's face. She stared at her sneakers.

Her father said, "Funny girl? What do you mean?"

Mrs. Graham laughed. "You'll never believe how this young lady fooled me last night. Kept telling me I had to stop seeing her father. That he didn't really care for me, that he was just putting me on."

"Tessa!" Her father's voice was sharp. "Tessa, what is this? What made you say such things?"

Tessa looked up at him, red-faced but determined. "I had to!" she said loudly. "I had to! Because you don't know what you're doing, Papá! You're under a spell!"

"Oh, no," Mrs. Graham said. "Is she . . . is she *your* daughter?"

"That's right," Papá said in a stern voice. "I'm sorry to have to admit it, but this funny girl is mine."

Tessa turned her face away. Papá's ashamed of me. Papá's sorry I'm his daughter. He did not even want to admit it. Hot tears stung her eyes and started to spill over. She turned on her heels and ran.

Chapter Fourteen

"**T**essa!" her father shouted, but she kept on running.

She had to go where she could hide her face, where she could not hear his words. *He hated to admit she was his daughter!* She raced by a group of people standing near the furthermost part of the bleachers. "Tessa, dear," a soft voice called, "are you all right?" It was Mrs. Herriot.

Tessa brushed tears away with the back of her hand and hurried around the end of the bleachers, searching for a place to hide. Footsteps pounded behind her. "Hey, Tessa," Wendell shouted, "what's wrong?"

"Stop chasing me!" she growled and looked around wildly for somewhere to be alone. Three metal trash cans stood below the bleachers between two metal supports. She dove behind them.

"Tessa!" Wendell called as he ran by her hiding place.

She waited until the sound of his footsteps had faded, then pushed deeper under the seats. The bleachers on this end of the field were empty; there were scattered patches of dim twilight sliding through the open spaces between the bench seats. Holding onto a metal crosspiece, she bent her head and huddled in the darkest corner. She squirmed as she thought about her father. If he hates me now, he'll hate me even more when he learns about the spell. The tears really started then and she let them roll down her cheeks. Finally, with a long, shaky sigh, she wiped her eyes and blew her nose.

It was darker now. She glanced at the sky through an open place above her. As she did, the full moon that was round as a Halloween pumpkin, slid from behind a cloud. Last month I could not wait for the moon to be round so that the rose potion would be ready. I wish I had never heard of a rose potion. Everything I have done is wrong. Everything I have tried is wrong. When a voice came over the public address system, she jumped, almost hitting her head on the boards above her.

"Ladies and gentlemen," a man said. "Hasn't this been great?" There was applause and cheers. When they quieted down, the man at the mike went on. "There's more to come. The awards program will begin in less than one hour. So don't leave early. You'll miss the best part of the fair if you do." He went on to make more announcements and when he was through, Tessa heard voices calling her.

"Tessa! Tess-a-a-a!" She recognized the calls. Haley. Mark. Let them call. I will come out when I'm ready, and I'm not ready yet.

She looked around. There was nothing to see but the trash cans that made a dark huddled mass near the open side of the bleachers and to her right, the mottled darkness that stretched down the length of the bleachers. There was nothing to hear but occasional voices and the bustling sound of movement overhead. As she watched, there was a scurrying sound near the cans and something moved. Maybe a dog, she thought, and shrunk back under the seats, not daring to breathe. Almost immediately, she realized that what she had seen was a person, not a dog.

"In here," someone said in a hoarse whisper. "Come on in here."

Tessa pressed deeper into her corner as two men scurried under the bleachers. They fell to their hands and knees and crawled under the lower seats to her right. They'll see me, she thought, pretty soon they'll see me. But in a moment she saw that they were not looking her way but at something they had put on the ground between them.

"Don't dump it, stupid!" one man hissed. "Something might make noise."

"Well, light a match then."

"You think it's safe?"

"Sure. I'll move around and cover you. Nobody'll see it."

The first man wriggled and dug in his pants' pocket. There was the scratch of a match and then a flickering yellow light lit up their faces and the object between them. Tessa recognized two things at once: they were not grown men, more like two high school guys, and the object they were looking at was a large woven purse.

They're thieves, Tessa thought with a shudder. I cannot let them find me here. They might have a gun and kill me!

"Jee-eez!" the first boy hissed as the match went out, obviously burning his fingertips.

"Light another!"

When the second match was lit, the second boy said, "Fat city! There are sixty bucks here!"

"How about credit cards?"

"We'll check in a minute. We've got house keys and an address. Let's go take a look at what's there."

"We don't have time."

"Who says? They're not gonna close the booths for a while and then there's the awards stuff. Besides, the old lady hasn't missed her purse yet, or we'd know it. So gimme more light. Let's see what else is here."

Another match flamed up and the boys fumbled through the purse again.

Tessa's hands were clammy, her mouth dry. They were going to break into someone's house! She drew in her breath and almost choked.

"Hey! Who's there?" The two boys turned her way. "Who's over there?"

Tessa's heart had been hammering against her chest. Now it bounced into her throat. "Help," she hollered, but only a squeak came through. Run, she told herself, you'd better run. For an instant her feet felt too heavy to lift, then, suddenly, they were moving, pushing her, along with her hands and knees, out of her corner toward the open end of the bleachers. There were scurrying sounds behind her and then a thud and a loud curse as someone's head hit the bottom of the seats. She pushed herself upright but as she did a hand grazed her back, pushing her off balance. Stumbling, she took two or three quick steps and fell headlong into the open. Hands pulled at her feet as she struggled to get up. "Stop it!" she screamed. "You're ruining my new shorts!"

"Shut up!" the boy at her feet whispered and pulled harder.

She clawed the ground. "Stop it! Stop it!" she screamed. "He-e-elp! Thieves! Help!"

"Tessa! Is that you?" Never had Wendell been more welcome. "What's . . . hey, leave her alone! Mark, help! I've found Tessa! Mark!"

Now above Tessa there seemed to be an explosion of arms and legs and curses and groans. Someone tripped over her, falling to the ground beside her. Wendell. "Mr. del Campo!" he yelled as he pulled one of the thieves down beside him. "Mr. del Campo! I've found Tessa!"

Things were calming down forty-five minutes later. The boys who stole the purse were taken away by the police. Mrs. Peters, the lady from whom the purse had been taken, went along to claim it and press charges. Wendell and Mark, who had been told by everyone that they were heroes, even though a couple of men helped them, went to the gym to clean up. And Tessa was left to face her father.

"Well," he said. "This is a night of surprises. And it isn't over yet. The important thing, though, is that those hoodlums didn't hurt you. Sure you're all right?"

Everyone had asked that. Her father had been first. Her mother, her long skirt held high, came running and asked the same thing. After that, it was the policemen. This was the third time for her father. Nita also asked.

"I'm fine, Papá," Tessa said impatiently. "All I did was trip. Wendell and Mark did the fighting."

"I know, I know," he said heartily. "They're good boys." Then his voice changed. "All right, Teresa, follow me. We have some quick talking to do." He led the way to a picnic table and sat down.

"I'm not sure what you were up to last night," he said, "but if it was a game—"

"It wasn't! I told her so!"

He shook his head. "I can hardly believe this. Well, why did you get a strange idea about Margaret Graham and I, I'll tell you, Teresa, I'm not going to allow you to—"

"It's not an idea, Papá! You're under a spell! That's what's happening! You're bewitched!"

Her father sighed. "So that's what it is. You think Mrs. Graham has me under her spell."

"Oh, no! No, no, no!" Tessa said, shaking her head briskly. "It's me! Not Ms. Graham. Me."

"Hm-m-mph." Her father straightened up and tightened his arms across his chest. There was a long moment of silence as he stared at her. He cleared his throat to speak, but a loud blare from the public address system stopped him.

"Miguel del Campo! Miguel del Campo! You're needed on the stage. *Now, Mike.* We need you right now."

Her father stood up. "All right, Tessa," he said. "We'll talk later. See what you can do about your appearance and come with me."

Chapter Fifteen

Her father handed Tessa a comb as they walked back to the bleachers. The comb helped her hair a little—only two or three snarls were left. But the rest of her was beyond help. Especially her white shorts. They were coverd with mud and dirt and something greasy green.

"I'm a real mess," Tessa said, leaning over to rub a scraped knee. "I'll go wait in the car."

"Definitely not," her father said and took her hand firmly.

Two rows of folding chairs had been set in a semi-circle close to the raised platform where the awards were to be made. Mamá, Nana María, and Nita were seated in the front row. Papá gave Tessa a gentle shove. "Go sit with your mother," he said.

"Yuck," Nita said when Tessa came near her. "You're an awful mess."

"Leave your sister alone," Mamá whispered and patted Tessa's arm.

"Why are we sitting here?" Tessa asked.

Mamá shook her head. "I'm not sure. I wanted to take you home, but your father insisted that we stay. So here we are."

Tessa leaned over to her grandmother and said, "Nana María, your son's acting totally mean tonight. He wouldn't listen to me either, and I want to go home." She fought back tears when Nana María patted her knee.

"Be patient, Teresita," her grandmother said. "*Cálmate.* Your father knows what he's doing." Tessa shrugged, sighed, and huddled back in her chair.

Two men and two women were seated on the platform. One was Mrs. Graham. Tessa's mouth dropped open as she saw her father walk across the platform and whisper something in her ear. He walked off quickly and came and sat beside Mamá. Then Mrs. Graham took the microphone.

She announced that this year the Merchants' Club was giving its first Citizen's Career Award to the person with the most excellent record. "We believe," she said, "that performance should be measured not only by achievement, but by dedication, constancy, and creativity."

Tessa squirmed. Boring, she thought, totally boring. This is going to be worse than last night's speeches. But, at least, Mrs. Graham was not talking long.

Mrs. Graham called the name of the third-place winner. It was Dr. Johnston, who was everybody's family doctor, so there was a lot of applause when he ran onto the platform and got a medal. Second place was given to a man named Karenbaum. Papá whispered that he was a marine biologist and a very important man.

A balloon popped. Tessa turned and, craning her neck, saw Mark and Wendell standing on the top row of the bleachers. They were holding bunches of balloons. It would be such fun to be with them. "Papá," she whispered, "why can't I—"

"Be still, Tessa," he ordered. "Listen to this."

"And now, our first-place winner is," Mrs. Graham was saying. There was a funny fluttering sound as everyone took a breath and waited. "Will Mrs. Claudia Flores del Campo please come up to the platform?"

Tessa gasped.

Mamá said, *"Wha-at?"*

Papá stood up. "Come on, Claudia," he said with a big grin. "This is it. We'll be right back, family."

Things are happening too fast, Tessa thought as she watched them go. Too fast and too hard to believe! There was *her very own mother* walking across the stage, flushed and smiling. Then there was Mrs. Graham's voice as she said, "For dedication to a noble career, homemaking, our first annual award is given . . ." Homemaking! How could that be? Next, there was the Merchants' Club president saying, "A homemaker must have the skills of a teacher, a nurse, a psychologist, and a CEO, plus the patience of a saint." They're talking about Mamá and all the things she does. They absolutely mean Mamá!

On top of everything, there was Nita, jumping up and down and making a pest of herself, not letting Tessa hear what the president was saying as he handed Mamá an envelope.

Suddenly, though, Tessa was aware of only one thing. That one thing seemed to happen in slow motion. Mrs. Graham got up and floated to the mike. There, with unbelievable slowness, she held up a thin black box. Carefully, she took a chain from the box and, inch by inch, brought it down over Mamá's neck. As she did, something brilliant sparkled in the lights.

Tessa's heart bounced into her throat. Then it dropped with a thud into her stomach. *It's the same box, the same shining jewel I saw Papá hand to Mrs. Graham! Everything is totally mixed up.* When Mamá hugged Mrs. Graham, Tessa slid slowly down in her chair. *What was going on?*

Mrs. Graham was talking again, telling where Mamá had gone to school and how she had given up her music to make a home. Behind Tessa a woman shouted, "Way to go, Claudia!" and everyone started clapping and yelling. Soon everyone was standing.

"Nita, stand up!" Tessa said, pulling her sister to her feet. "This is all for Mamá!" And because she would have exploded if she had not, she gave Nita a great big hug.

Dear Diary,

   It's Sunday, 11:30 p.m.! Imagine it! Old sleepy-head me is still wide awake. Well, you would be too. So much has happened. It all started when we got to the fairgrounds . . .

   . . . After Mamá got the medal Papá came down and dragged Nita and me up on to the stage. I mean *dragged*. Well, not Nita. *She* was all ready to show off her dumb pink frills. But I was a total scuzz. Mud and snarls and scrapes. I thought I would die. But I didn't because here I am. You know what Mrs. Graham did? She told everyone that I had saved Mrs. Peters' house from being broken into. I blushed. All over. My toes included. But I had the sense to remind her that Wendell and Mark had a lot to do with it and she announced their names too. That's when a lot of balloons popped. Guess who did that?

But here's the big news! The envelope Mamá was given is a prize. It has a certificate for a trip to be taken the first two weeks in August. She gets to pick between a Caribbean or a Panama Canal cruise. Mamá says we can vote which one tomorrow. Because it's for the whole family! Another thing, diary. Papá told me that he found out that Mamá was the winner of the trip right after he'd said yes to my summer with Lisa. So that's why he couldn't let me go. He couldn't explain because he'd made a promise not to tell anyone. Boy, he can really keep a secret, can't he? Just like Nana María. I guess that's where we both get it.

There's one thing I haven't figured out yet. But I'm too tired to think about it tonight. Did the backwards spell work? Is that why things turned out so great? Am I still a witch?

Chapter Sixteen

In the arbor the next afternoon Tessa told Mark about the trip.

"We're still trying to decide," she said. "The Caribbean or Panama. Which do you think is most mysterious?"

Mark shrugged. "They just sound a little foreign to me."

"Well, that's mysterious, isn't it?"

"Everything's mysterious to you."

"Maybe it is," she said, frowning. Pretty soon she said, "Remember the backwards spell I did on my father?"

"Sure I remember. You just told me yesterday. What about it?"

"Do you think it worked?"

Mark breathed in air way down to his middle, then let it out. "How could it work?" he said impatiently. "There never was a spell to begin with."

Tessa sighed. "That's what Papá said this morning when we talked."

"Holy cow! You mean you told him we spied on him?"

"I didn't have to. He didn't ask me anything. Not even about the magic spell. Just said he wanted me to understand *once and for all* and told me not to interrupt. Then he explained why he'd been meeting with Mrs. Graham and why it had to be a secret."

"That's easy," Mark said. "I figured it out last night. He had to tell her all about your mom. How else could Mrs. Graham know where your mom went to school and about her music and things? And if he told anybody— even you—your mom would be sure to find out."

"I know," Tessa said sadly. "Still . . . don't you think . . . couldn't my spell have had *something* to do with it?"

"You never give up, do you? What's so special about being a dumb witch? Which you aren't, anyway."

"Who says?"

"I do. Look, if you still think you can, go ahead, put a spell on me."

Her face got hot. "I could, I guess," she said, "but I don't want to."

"Okay, be a witch. Wendell and I are going to be private investigators."

"Wendell and you? Since when?"

"Since last night. The arbor's going to be our center of operations."

Tessa swallowed hard. Mark had been here only a few weeks and he was taking over everything! Wendell had always been *her* friend. And now, everybody was going to know about the arbor! "I'll bet you told him how to get in my special way."

"Not yet. But I'm going to. We've got to start our business while everybody still remembers that we caught the purse thieves."

"*Without me?* I'm the one who really caught them!"

Mark rolled his eyes toward the sky. "Holy cow, Tessa! Are you a witch or aren't you? Make up your mind."

Monday night.

Dear diary,

. . . so you see when Mark said to make up my mind, I just had to. I wanted to tell him how exciting it is to have magic powers, how I'd been looking forward to all the spells on my "to do" list, especially the one about getting the fun arcade for us kids, but I couldn't. Mark may be smart, but what does he know about being a witch? He doesn't even think they exist.

I personally think there are. At least a few. That's why I'm going to resign by letter. I want them to know I'm serious. I'll put the letter next to the spot where I put the old pages of recipes and rites. (That's the first place I'd look if I was in charge of witches.) Here it goes. It better be all right.

> To Whom It May Concern in Covens and Other Places:
>
> It is hereby announced that María Teresa del Campo, also known as Tessa, resigns here and now from the great sisterhood of witches to which she belonged for such a little bit. Said María Teresa del Campo promises that during the next full moon all magic tools of her trade will be buried in a secret place, never to be dug up, especially the rose potion. Also please resign the cat, Homer, from his duties as a witch's "familiar."

There, diary, I've done it. Now I can be a private investigator. Starting right now I am a member of Tracers International. Personally, I never was worried that Mark and Wendell would go into business without me. They'd be scared I might put a spell on them.

Additional Young Adult Titles

A School Named For Someone Like Me
Diana Dávila Martínez
2004, Trade Paperback
ISBN 1-55885-334-0, $9.95

Across the Great River
Irene Beltrán Hernández
1989, Trade Paperback
ISBN 0-934770-96-4, $9.95

Alicia's Treasure
Diane Gonzales Bertrand
1996, Trade Paperback
ISBN 1-55885-086-4, $7.95

Ankiza
A Roosevelt High School Series Book
Gloria Velásquez
2000, Clothbound
ISBN 1-55885-308-1, $16.95
Trade Paperback
ISBN 1-55885-309-X, $9.95

*¡Aplauso! Hispanic Children's
Theater*
Edited by Joe Rosenberg
1995, Trade Paperback
ISBN 1-55885-127-5, $12.95

*Bailando en silencio: Escenas de
una niñez puertorriqueña*
Judith Ortiz Cofer, Translated by
Elena Olazagasti-Segovia
1997 Trade Paperback
ISBN 1-55885-205-0, $12.95

Border Crossing
Maria Colleen Cruz
2003, Trade Paperback
ISBN 1-55885-405-3, $9.95

Call Me Consuelo
Ofelia Dumas Lachtman
1997, Trade Paperback
ISBN 1-55885-187-9, $9.95

Close to the Heart
Diane Gonzales Bertrand
2002, Trade Paperback
ISBN 1-55885-319-7, $9.95

Creepy Creatures and Other Cucuys
Xavier Garza
2004, Trade Paperback
ISBN 1-55885-410-X, $9.95

*Dionicio Morales: A Life in
Two Cultures*
Dionicio Morales
1997, Trade Paperback
ISBN 1-55885-219-0, $9.95

Don't Spit On My Corner
Mike Durán
1992, Trade Paperback
ISBN 1-55885-042-2, $9.50

Emilio
Julia Mercedes Castilla
1999, Trade Paperback
ISBN 1-55885-271-9, $9.95

Firefly Summer
Pura Belpré
1997, Trade Paperback
ISBN 1-55885-180-1, $9.95

Fitting In
Anilú Bernardo
1996, Trade Paperback
ISBN 1-55885-173-9, $9.95

From Amigos to Friends
Pelayo "Pete" Garcia
1997, Trade Paperback
ISBN 1-55885-207-7, $7.95

*The Ghostly Rider and Other
Chilling Stories*
Hernán Moreno-Hinojosa
2003, Trade Paperback
ISBN 1-55885-400-2, $9.95

A Good Place for Maggie
Ofelia Dumas Lachtman
2002, Trade Paperback
ISBN 1-55885-372-3, $9.95

The Girl from Playa Blanca
Ofelia Dumas Lachtman
1995, Trade Paperback
ISBN 1-55885-149-6, $9.95

Heartbeat Drumbeat
Irene Beltrán Hernández
1992, Trade Paperback,
ISBN 1-55885-052-X, $9.50

Hispanic, Female and Young:
An Anthology
Edited by Phyllis Tashlik
1994, Trade Paperback
ISBN 1-55885-080-5, $14.95

The Ice Dove and Other Stories
Diane de Anda
1997, Trade Paperback
ISBN 1-55885-189-5, $7.95

The Immortal Rooster and
Other Stories
Diane de Anda
1999, Trade Paperback
ISBN 1-55885-278-6, $9.95

In Nueva York
Nicholasa Mohr
1993, Trade Paperback
ISBN 0-934770-78-6, $10.95

Juanita Fights the School Board
A Roosevelt High School Series Book
Gloria Velásquez
1994, Trade Paperback
ISBN 1-55885-115-1, $9.95

Julian Nava: My Mexican-American
Journey
Julian Nava
2002, Clothbound
ISBN 1-55885-364-2, $16.95

Jumping Off to Freedom
Anilú Bernardo
1996, Trade Paperback
ISBN 1-55885-088-0, $9.95

Lessons of the Game
Diane Gonzales Bertrand
1998, Trade Paperback
ISBN 1-55885-245-X, $9.95

Leticia's Secret
Ofelia Dumas Lachtman
1997, Trade Paperback
ISBN 1-55885-209-3, $7.95
Clothbound, ISBN 1-55885-208-5, $14.95

Looking for La Única
Ofelia Dumas Lachtman
2004, Trade Paperback
ISBN 1-55885-412-6, $9.95

Lorenzo's Revolutionary Quest
Rick and Lila Guzmán
2003, Trade Paperback
ISBN 1-55885-392-8, $9.95

Lorenzo's Secret Mission
Rick and Lila Guzmán
2001, Trade Paperback
ISBN 1-55885-341-3, $9.95

Loves Me, Loves Me Not
Anilú Bernardo
1998, Trade Paperback
ISBN 1-55885-259-X, $9.95

The Making of a Civil Rights Leader:
José Angel Gutiérrez
José Angel Gutiérrez
2005, Trade Paperback
ISBN 1-55885-451-7, $9.95

Maya's Divided World
A Roosevelt High School
Series Book
Gloria Velásquez
1995, Trade Paperback
ISBN 1-55885-131-3, $9.95

Mexican Ghost Tales
Alfred Avila
Edited by Kat Avila
1994, Trade Paperback
ISBN 1-55885-107-0, $9.95

My Own True Name
New and Selected Poems for
Young Adults, 1984-1999
Pat Mora
Drawings by Anthony Accardo
2000, Trade Paperback
ISBN 1-55885-292-1, $11.95

Nilda
Nicholasa Mohr
1986, Trade Paperback
ISBN 0-934770-61-1, $11.95

*Orange Candy Slices and
    Other Secret Tales*
Viola Canales
2001, Trade Paperback
ISBN 1-55885-332-4, $9.95

The Orlando Cepeda Story
Bruce Markusen
2001, Clothbound
ISBN 1-55885-333-2, $16.95

Pillars of Gold and Silver
Beatriz de la Garza
1997, Trade Paperback
ISBN 1-55885-206-9,$9.95

*Riding Low on the Streets of Gold:
    Latino Literature for Young Adults*
Edited by Judith Ortiz Cofer
2003, Trade Paperback
ISBN 1-55885-380-4, $14.95

Rina's Family Secret
    A Roosevelt High School Series Book
Gloria Velásquez
1998, Trade Paperback
ISBN 1-55885-233-6,$9.95

Roll Over, Big Toben
Victor Sandoval
2003, Trade Paperback
ISBN 1-55885-401-0, $9.95

The Secret of Two Brothers
Irene Beltrán Hernández
1995, Trade Paperback
ISBN 1-55885-142-9, $9.95

*Silent Dancing: A Partial
    Remembrance of a Puerto
    Rican Childhood*
Judith Ortiz Cofer
1991, Trade Paperback
ISBN 1-55885-015-5,92.95

Spirits of the High Mesa
Floyd Martínez
1997, Trade Paperback
ISBN 1-55885-198-4, $9.95

The Summer of El Pintor
Ofelia Dumas Lachtman
2001, Trade Paperback
ISBN 1-55885-327-8, $9.95

Sweet Fifteen
Diane Gonzales Bertrand
1995, Trade Paperback
ISBN 1-55885-133-X, $9.95

*The Tall Mexican: The Life of
    Hank Aguirre, All-Star Pitcher,
    Businessman, Humanitarian*
Bob Copley
1998, Trade Paperback
ISBN 1-55885-294-8,$9.95

*Teaching through Culture: Strategies
    for Reading and Responding to
    Young Adult Literature*
Joan Parker Webster
2002, Trade Paperback
ISBN 1-55885-376-6, $16.95

Teen Angel
    A Roosevelt High School Series Book
Gloria Velásquez
2003, Trade Paperback
ISBN 1-55885-391-X, $9.95

Tommy Stands Alone
    A Roosevelt High School Series Book
Gloria Velásquez
1995, Clothbound
ISBN 1-55885-146-1, $14.95
Trade Paperback
ISBN 1-55885-147-X, $9.95

Trino's Choice
Diane Gonzales Bertrand
1999, Trade Paperback
ISBN 1-55885-268-9, $9.95

Trino's Time
Diane Gonzales Bertrand
2001, Clothbound
ISBN 1-55885-316-2, $14.95
Trade Paperback
ISBN 1-55885-317-0, $9.95

Upside Down and Backwards
Diane Gonzales Bertrand
2004, Tradeback
ISBN 1-55885-408-8, $9.95

Versos sencillos/Simple Verses
José Martí, Translated by Manuel A.
Tellechea
1997, Trade Paperback
ISBN 1-55885-204-2, $12.95,

Viaje a la tierra del abuelo
Mario Bencastro
2004, Trade Paperback
ISBN 1-55885-404-5, $9.95

Walking Stars
Victor Villaseñor
2003, Trade Paperback
ISBN 1-55885-394-4, $10.95

White Bread Competition
Jo Ann Yolanda Hernandez
1997, Trade Paperback
ISBN 1-55885-210-7, $9.95

The Year of Our Revolution
Judith Ortiz Cofer
1998, Trade Paperback
ISBN 1-55885-224-7, $16.95

...y no se lo trago la tierra
Tomás Rivera
1996, Trade Paperback
ISBN 1-55885-151-8, $7.95